THOMAS BAILEY ALDRICH

Two Bites at a Cherry, with Other Tales

The American Short Story Series

VOLUME 34

GARRETT PRESS

512-00006-9

Library of Congress Catalog Card No. 69-11877

*This volume was reprinted from the 1894 edition
published by Houghton-Mifflin (Riverside Press)*

First Garrett Press Edition published 1969

The American Short Story Series
Volume 34
©1969

Manufactured in the United States of America

GARRETT PRESS, INC.
Publishers

250 West 54th Street, New York, N.Y. 10019

CONTENTS

TWO BITES AT A CHERRY

I

As they both were Americans, and typical Americans, it ought to have happened in their own country. But destiny has no nationality, and consequently no patriotism ; so it happened in Naples.

When Marcus Whitelaw strolled out of his hotel that May morning, and let himself drift with the crowd along the Strada del Duomo until he reached the portals of the ancient cathedral, nothing was more remote from his meditation than Mrs. Rose Mason. He had not seen her for fifteen years, and he had not thought of her, except in an intermittent fashion, for seven or eight. There had, however, been a period, covering possibly four years, when he had thought of little else. During that heavy interim he had gone about with a pain in his bosom — a pain that had been very keen at the beginning, and then had gradually lost its edge. Later on, that invisible hand which obliterates even the deep-carved grief on headstones effectually smoothed out the dent in Whitelaw's heart.

Rose Jenness at nineteen had been singularly adapted to making dents in certain kinds of hearts. Her candor and unselfishness, her disdain of insincerity in others, and her unconsciousness of the spells she cast had proved more fatal to Whitelaw than the most studied coquetry would have done. In the deepest stress of his trouble he was denied the consolation of being able to reproach her with duplicity. He had built up his leaning tower of hopes without any aid from her. She had been nothing but frank and unmisleading from first to last. Her beauty she could not help. She came of a line of stately men and handsome women. Sir Peter Lely painted them in Charles the Second's time, and Copley found them ready for his canvas at the close of the colonial period. Through some remote cross of Saxon and Latin blood, the women of this family had always been fair and the men dark. In Rose Jenness the two characteristics flowered. When New England produces a blonde with the eyes of a brunette, the world cannot easily match her, especially if she have that rounded slenderness of figure which is one of our very best Americanisms.

Without this blended beauty, which came to perfection in her suddenly, like the blossoms on a fruit-tree, Whitelaw would have loved Rose all the same. Indeed, her physical loveliness had counted for little in his passion, though the loveliness had afterwards haunted him almost maliciously. That she was fair of person who had so many gracious traits of mind and disposition was a matter of course. He had been slower than others in detecting the charm that wrapt her as she slipped into womanhood. They had grown up together as children, and had known no separation, except during the three years White-

law was with the Army of the Potomac —
an absence broken by several returns to
the North on recruiting service, and one
long sojourn after a dangerous hurt received at Antietam. He never knew when
he began to love Rose, and he never knew
the exact moment when he ceased to love
her. But between these two indefinable
points he had experienced an unhappiness
that was anything but indefinite. It had
been something tangible and measurable ;
and it had changed the course of his career.

Next to time, there is no surer medicine
than hard work for the kind of disappointment we have indicated. Unfortunately
for Whitelaw, he was moderately rich by
inheritance, and when he discovered that
Rose's candid affection was not love, he
could afford to indulge his wretchedness.
He had been anxious for distinction, for
her sake ; but now his ambition was gone.
Of what value to him were worldly prizes,
if she refused to share them ? He presently withdrew from the legal profession,
in which he had given promise of becom-

ing a brilliant pleader, who had pleaded so unsuccessfully for himself, and went abroad. This was of course after the war.

It was not her fault that all communication between them ceased then and there. He would have it so. The affair had not been without its bitterness for Rose. Whitelaw was linked in some way with every agreeable reminiscence of her life; she could not remember the time when she was not fond of him. There had been a poignancy in the regret with which she had seen the friend who was dear to her transforming himself into a lover for whom she did not care in the least. It had pained her to give him pain, and she had done it with tears in her eyes.

Eighteen months later, Rose was Mrs. Mason, tears and all. Richard Mason was a Pacific Railway king *en herbe*, with a palace in San Francisco, whither he immediately transported his bride. The news reached Whitelaw in Seville, and gave him a twinge. His love, according to his own diagnosis, was already dead; it was presumably, then, a muscular contraction that caused it to turn a little in its coffin. The following year some question of investment brought him back to the United States, where he travéled extensively, carefully avoiding California. He visited Salt Lake City, however, and took cynical satisfaction in observing what a large amount of connubial misery there was to the square foot. Yet when a rumor came to him, some time subsequently, that Rose herself was not very happy in her marriage, he had the grace to be sincerely sorry.

" The poor transplanted Rose ! " he murmured. " She was too good for him ; she was too good for anybody."

This was four years after she had refused to be his wife ; time had brought the philosophic mind, and he could look back upon the episode with tender calmness, and the desire to do justice to every one. Meanwhile Rose had had a boy. Whitelaw's feelings in respect to him were complicated.

Seven or eight years went by, the greater part of which Whitelaw passed in England.

There he heard nothing of Mrs. Mason, and when in America he heard very little. The marriage had not been fortunate, the Masons were enormously wealthy, and she was a beauty still. The Delaneys had met her, one winter, at Santa Barbara. Her letters home had grown more and more infrequent, and finally ceased. Her father had died, and the family was broken up and scattered. People whom nobody knew occupied the old mansion on the slope of Beacon Hill. One of the last spells of the past was lifted for Whitelaw when he saw strange faces looking out of those sun-purpled window-panes.

If Whitelaw thought of Mrs. Mason at intervals, it was with less distinctness on each occasion ; the old love-passage, when he recalled it of an evening over his cigar, or in the course of some solitary walk, had a sort of phantasmal quality about it. The sharp grief that was to have lasted forever had resolved itself into a painless memory. He was now on that chilly side of forty where one begins to take ceremonious leave of one's illusions, and prefers Burgundy to champagne.

When the announcement of Richard Mason's death was telegraphed East, Whitelaw read the telegram in his morning paper with scarcely more emotion than was shown by the man who sat opposite him reading the particulars of the last homicide. This was in a carriage on the Sixth Avenue elevated railway, for Whitelaw chanced to be in New York at the moment, making preparations for an extended tour in Russia and its dependencies. The Russian journey proved richer in novelty than he had anticipated, and he remained nearly three years in the land of the Tsars. On returning to Western Europe he was seized with the humor to revisit certain of the Italian cities,— Ravenna, Rome, Venice, and Naples. It was in Naples that he found himself on that particular May morning to which reference has been made.

Whitelaw had never before happened to be in the city during the *festa* of San Gennaro. There are three of these festivals

annually — in May, September, and December. He had fallen upon the most picturesque of the series. The miracle of the
Liquefaction of the Blood of St. Januarius
was to take place at nine o'clock that forenoon in the cathedral, and it was a specta-
cle which Whitelaw had often desired to
witness.

So it was that he followed the crowd
along the sunny *strada*, and shouldered his
way into the church, where the great can-
dles were already lighted. The cool atmosphere of the interior, pleasantly touched
with that snuffy, musky odor which haunts
Italian churches, was refreshing after the
incandescent heat outside. He did not
mind being ten or twelve minutes too early.

Whitelaw had managed to secure a position not far from the altar-rail, and was
settling himself comfortably to enjoy the
ceremony, with his back braced against a
marble column, when his eyes fell upon the
profile of a lady who was standing about
five yards in advance of him in an oblique
line.

II

For an instant that face seemed to Whitelaw a part of the theatric unreality which always impresses one in Roman Catholic churches abroad. The sudden transition from the white glare of the street into the semi-twilight of the spacious nave; the soft bloom of the stained windows; the carving and gilding of choir and reredos; the draperies and frescoes, and the ghostly forms of incense slowly stretching upward, like some of Blake's weird shapes, to blend themselves with the shadows among the Gothic arches — all these instantly conspire to lift one from the commonplace level of life. With such accessories, and in certain moods, the mind pliantly surrenders itself to the incredible.

During possibly thirty seconds, Whitelaw might have been mistaken for the mate of one of those half-length figures in alto-relievo set against the neighboring pilasters, so grotesque and wooden was his expression. Then he gave a perceptible start. That gold hair, in waves of its own on the low brows, the sombre eyelashes — he could not see her eyes from where he stood — the poise of the head, the modeling of the throat — who could that be but Rose Jenness? He had involuntarily eliminated the Mason element, for the sight of her had taken him straight back to the days when there were no Pacific Railway despots.

Fifteen years (good heavens! was it fifteen years?) had not touched a curve of the tall, slight figure. He was struck by that, as she stood there with her satin basque buttoned up to the thread-lace neckerchief knotted under her chin, for an insidious chill lurked in the air. The garment fitted closely, accentuating every line of the slender waist and flower-like full bust. At the left of the corsage was a bunch of violets held by a small silver clasp — the selfsame violets, he was tempted to believe, that she had worn the evening he parted with her tragically in the back drawing-room of the house on Beacon Hill. Neither she nor they had faded. All the details of that parting flashed upon him with strange vividness: the figure-piece by Hunt above the funereal fireplace; the crimson India shawl hurriedly thrown over the back of a chair and trailing on the floor; Rose standing in the middle of the dimly-lighted room and holding out to him an appealing hand, which he refused to take. He remembered noticing, as he went home dazed through the moonlight, that the crisp crocuses were in bloom in the little front yards of the houses on Mount Vernon Street. It was May then, and it was May now, and there stood Rose. As he gazed at her, a queer sense of old comradeship — the old friendship that had gone to sleep when love awakened — began softly to stir in his bosom.

Rose in Italy! Then he recollected one of the past rumors that had floated to him touching her desire for foreign travel, and Mason's sordid absorption in his railway schemes. Now that she was untrammeled,

she had come abroad. She had probably
left home with her son soon after Mason's
death, and had been flitting from one con-
tinental city to another ever since, in the
tiresome American fashion. That might
well have befallen without Whitelaw hearing of it in Russia. The lists of new arriv-
als were the things he avoided in reading
Galignani, just as he habitually avoided the
newly-arrived themselves.

There was no hesitation in his mind as to
the course he should pursue. The moment
he could move he would go to Rose, and
greet her without embarrassment or any
arrière pensée. It was impracticable to
move at present, for the people were packed
about him as solidly as dates in a crate.
Meanwhile he had the freedom of his eyes.
He amused himself with recognizing and
classifying one by one certain evidences of
individuality in Rose's taste in the matter
of dress. The hat, so subdued in color and
sparing of ornament as to make it a mystery
where the rich effect came from — there was
a great deal of her in that. He would have

identified it at once as Rose's hat if he had picked it up in the Desert of Sahara. Noting this, and the long tan-colored gloves which reached in wrinkles to the elbow, and would have reached to the shoulder if they had been drawn out smooth, Whitelaw murmured to himself, "Rue de la Paix!" He had a sensation of contiguity to a pair of high-heeled kid boots with rosettes at the instep, such as are worn in all weathers by aristocratic shepherdesses in Watteau's pink landscapes. That, however, was an unprovoked incursion into the territory of conjecture, for Whitelaw could see only the upper portion of Rose.

He was glad, since accident had thrown them together, that accident had not done it in the first twelvemonth of Rose's widowhood. Any mortuary display on her part would, he felt, have jarred the wrong note in him, and spoiled the pleasure of meeting her. But she was out of mourning now; the man was dead, had been dead three years, and ought to have lived and died in the pterodactyl period, to which he properly belonged. Here Whitelaw paused in his musing, and smiled at his own heat, with a transient humorous perception of it. Let the man go; what was the use of thinking about him?

Dismissing the late Richard Mason, who really had not been a prehistoric monster, and had left Mrs. Mason a large fortune to do what she liked with, Whitelaw fell to thinking about Rose's son. He must be quite thirteen years old, our friend reflected. What an absurdly young-looking woman Rose was to be the mother of a thirteen-year-old boy! — doubtless a sad scapegrace, answering to the definition which Whitelaw remembered that one of his strong-minded country-women had given of the typical bad boy — a boy who looks like his mother and behaves like his father. Did Rose's son look like his mother?

Just then Rose slightly turned her head, and Whitelaw fancied that he detected an inquiring, vaguely anxious expression in her features, as if she were searching for some one in the assemblage. "She is looking for

young Mason," he soliloquized; which was
precisely the fact. She glanced over the
church, stared for an instant straight past
Whitelaw, and then resumed her former
position. He had prepared himself to meet
her gaze; but she had not seen him. And
now a tall Englishman, with a single eye-
glass that gleamed like a headlight, came
and planted himself, as if with malice pre-
pense, between the two Americans.

"The idiot!" muttered Whitelaw, between his teeth.

Up to the present point he had paid no
attention whatever to St. Januarius. The
apparition of his early love, in what might
be called the bloom of youth, was as much
miracle as he could take in at once. Moreover, the whole of her was here, and only a
fragment of the saint. Whitelaw was now
made aware, by an expectant surging of the
crowd in front and the craning of innumerable necks behind him, that something important was on the tapis.

A priest, in ordinary non-sacramental
costume, had placed on the altar, from

which all but the permanent decorations
had been removed, a life-size bust of St.
Januarius in gold and silver, inclosing the
remains of the martyr's skull. Having performed this act, the priest, who for the occasion represented the archbishop, took his
stand at the left of the dais. Immediately
afterwards a procession of holy fathers,
headed by acolytes bearing lighted candela-
bra, issued from behind the high altar,
where the saint's relics are kept in a taber-
nacle on off days and nights. An imposing
personage half-way down the file carried a
tall brass monstrance, in which was suspended by a ring an oblong flat crystal
flask, or case, set in an antique reliquary of
silver, with handles at each end. This contained the phenomenal blood.

Having deposited the monstrance on the
altar, the custodian reverently detached
the relic, and faced the audience. As he
held up the flask by the handles and slowly
turned it round, those nearest could distinguish through the blurred surface a dark
yellowish opaque substance, occupying about

two thirds of the vessel. It was apparently a solid mass, which in a liquid form might have filled a couple of sherry glasses. The legend runs that the thoughtful Roman lady who gathered the blood from the ground with a sponge inadvertently let drop a bit of straw into the original phial. This identical straw, which appears when the lump is in a state of solution, is considered a strong piece of circumstantial evidence. It is a remarkable fact, and one that by itself establishes the authenticity of San Gennaro, that several of his female descendants always assist at the liquefaction — a row of very aged and very untidy Neapolitan ladies, to whom places of honor are given on these occasions.

Shut out from Rose, for the obnoxious Englishman completely blockaded her, Whitelaw lent himself with faintly stimulated interest to the ceremony, which was now well under way. He was doubtful of many things, and especially skeptical as to matters supernatural. Accepting the miracle at its own valuation — at par value, as he stated it — what conceivable profit could accrue to mankind from the smelting of that poor old gentleman's coagulated blood? How had all this mediæval mummery survived the darkness in which it was born!

With half listless eye Whitelaw watched the priest as he stood at the rail, facing the spectators and solemnly reversing the reliquary. From time to time he paused, and held a lighted candle behind the flask in order to ascertain if any change had taken place, and then resumed operations amid the breathless silence. An atmosphere charged with suspense seemed to have settled upon the vast throng.

Six — eight — ten minutes passed. The priest had several times repeated his investigation; but the burnt-sienna-like mass held to its consistency. In life St. Januarius must have been a person of considerable firmness, a quality which his blood appeared still to retain even after the lapse of more than fourteen centuries.

A thrill of disappointment and dismay ran through the multitude. The miracle

was not working, in fact had refused to
work! The attendants behind the chancel
rail wore perturbed faces. Two of the
brothers turned to the altar and began saying the Athanasian Creed, while here and
there a half breathed prayer or a deep mut-
tering of protest took flight from the congregation; for the Neapolitans insist on a
certain degree of punctuality in St. Januarius. Any unreasonable delay on his part
is portentous of dire calamity to the city
— earthquake or pestilence. The least
that can be predicted is an eruption of
Mount Vesuvius. Even so late as the end
of the eighteenth century, a failure of the
miracle usually led to panic and violence.
To-day such a result is hardly possible,
though in the rare instances when the martyr procrastinates a little, the populace fall
to upbraiding their patron saint with a
vehemence that is quite as illogical in its
way.

Whitelaw himself was nearly ripe to
join in some such demonstration. Trans-
fixed to the marble column — like a second

St. Sebastian — and pierced with innumerable elbows, he had grown very impatient of the whole business. There was Rose within twenty feet of him, and he could neither approach her nor see her! He heartily wished that when Proconsul Dracontius threw St. Januarius to the lions in the amphitheatre of Pozzuoli, the lions had not left a shred of him, instead of tamely lapping his hand. Then Dracontius would not have been obliged to behead the man; then that Roman lady would not have come along with her sponge; then he, Marcus Whitelaw, a free-born American citizen, would not have been kept standing there a lifetime waiting for an opportunity to say a word to his old love!

He felt that he had much to say to Rose. The barrier which had separated him from her all these years had been swept away. The whole situation was essentially changed. If she were willing to accept the friendship which she once stipulated as the only tie possible between them, he was ready to offer it to her now. If she had not altered,

if she remained her old candid cordial self,
what a treat it would be to him to act as
her cicerone in Naples — for Naples was
probably *terra incognita* to Rose.   There
were delightful drives along the Riviere di
Chiaia; excursions to Pompeii, Baiæ, and
Solfatara; trips by steamer to Capri, Sor-
rento, and Amalfi.   He pictured the two of
of them drifting in a boat into the sappha-
rine enchantment of the Blue Grotto at
Capri — the three of them, rather; for
" By Jove ! " he reflected, " we should have
to take the boy with us."   This reflection
somewhat dashed his spirits.   The juvenile
Mason would be a little bore; and if he
did n't look like his mother, and *did* look
like his father, the youth would be a great
bore.

Now as Whitelaw had never seen the
late Mr. Mason, or even a counterfeit pre-
sentment of him, any resemblance that
might chance to exist between the father
and the son was not likely to prove aggressive.   This reflection also occurred to
Whitelaw, and caused him to smile.   He

had a touch of that national gift of humorous self-introspection which enables Americans, almost alone among human bipeds, to smile at their own expense.

While these matters were passing through his mind, and he had given up all hope of extricating himself from his predicament until the end of the ceremony, a sudden eddy swirled round the column, the crowd wavered and broke, and Whitelaw was free. The disintegration of the living mass was only momentary, but before it could close together again he had contrived to get three yards away from the site of his martyrdom. Further advance then became difficult. By dint of pushing and diplomatic elbowing he presently gained another yard. The goal was almost won.

A moment later he stood at Rose's side.

III

ROSE had her head turned three quarters to the right, and was unaware that any one had supplanted the tall English gentleman recently looming on her left. Whitelaw drew a long breath, and did not speak at once, but stood biting his under lip with an air of comic irresolution. He was painfully conscious that it was comic. He had, in fact, fallen into an absurd perplexity. How should he address her? He did not quite dare to call her "Rose," and every fibre of his being revolted against calling her "Mrs. Mason." Yet he must address her in some fashion, and instantly. There was one alternative — not to address her. He bent down a little, and touched her lightly on the shoulder.

The lady wheeled sharply, with a movement that must have been characteristic of her, and faced him. There was no faltering

or reservation in voice or manner as she exclaimed " Marc ! " and gave one of the tan-
colored gloves into his keeping for twenty
seconds or so. She had spoken rather loud,
forgetting circumstance and place in her
surprise, and several of the masculine bystanders smiled sympathetically on *la bella
Americana*. There was the old ring to her
voice, and it vibrated musically on Whitelaw's ear.

" Rose," he said, in an undertone, " I
cannot tell you how glad I am of this. I
begin to believe that things are planned for
me better than I can plan them."

" This was planned charmingly — but it
was odd to make us meet in Naples, when
we have so much room at home to meet in."

" The odd feature of it to me is that it
does n't appear odd. I don't see how anything else could have happened without
breaking all the laws of probability."

" It seems much too good to be true,"
said Rose gayly.

She was unaffectedly happy over the en-
counter, and the manner of it. She had

caused Whitelaw a deep mortification in days past, and though it had been the consequence of no fault of her own, had indeed been entirely Whitelaw's, she had always wanted the assurance of his forgiveness. That he had withheld through long years, and now he forgave her. She read the pardon in his voice and eyes. Rose scanned him a little curiously, though with no overt act of curiosity. He had grown stouter, but the added fullness was not unbecoming : he used to be too spare for his stature. His sharp New England face belonged to a type that seldom loses its angles. The scar in the shape of a cross on his left cheek was decorative. The handsomely moulded upper lip was better without the mustache. There were silvery glints here and there where the chestnut hair was brushed back from the temples. These first few scattering snowflakes of time went well with his bronzed complexion ; for he was as brown as an Indian, from travel. On the whole, fifteen years had decidedly adorned him.

"How long have you been here — in Naples, I mean?" questioned Whitelaw, again under his breath.

"A week; and you?"

"Since yesterday. I came chiefly for this *festa*."

"I did n't dream you were so devout."

"The conversion is recent; but henceforth I swear by St. Januarius through thick and thin, though as a general thing I prefer him thin — when it does n't take too long."

"If any one should hear you!" whispered Rose, glancing round furtively.

"Why, the church itself does n't cling very strongly to the miracle nowadays, and would gladly be rid of it; but the simple folk of the Santa Lucia quarter and the outlying volcanoes insist on having their St. Januarius. I imagine it would cost a revolution to banish him. Rose, when did you leave home?"

"Last March. Hush!" she added, laying a finger to her lip. "Something is happening in the chancel."

The martyr's blood had finally given
signs of taking the proper sanguine hue,
to the intense relief of the populace, from
which arose a dull multitudinous murmur,
like that of a distant swarm of bees. The
priest, with a gleam of beatific triumph in
his cavernous eyes, was holding the reliquary
high aloft. The vast congregation swayed
to and fro, and some tumult was created
by devotees in the background endeavoring to obtain coignes of vantage nearer the
altar.

"Surely, you have not trusted yourself
alone in this place?" said Whitelaw.

"No, I'm with you," Rose answered
smiling.

"But you did not come unattended?"

"Richard came with me; we got separated immediately on entering the cathedral,
and lost each other."

"Richard — that is the name of your
son," remarked Whitelaw, after a pause.
The father's name!

"Yes, and I want you to see him. He's
a fine fellow."

"I should like to see him," said White-law perfunctorily.

"He is very clever, not like me."

"I hope he's as unaware of his clever-ness as you are of yours, Rose."

"I am quite aware of mine. I only said that his was different. That spoils your compliment. He's to remain over here at school — in Germany — if I can make up my mind in the autumn to leave him. When do you return to America?"

"In the autumn," said Whitelaw, promptly, a little to his own surprise, for until then he really had had no plan.

"Perhaps we can arrange to go back on the same steamer," suggested Rose. "We crossed in the Cuba, and liked her. She's advertised to sail on the 17th of September; how would that suit you, for example?"

The suggestion smiled upon Whitelaw, and he was about to reply, when a peal from the great organ, announcing the consumma-tion of the miracle, reverberated through the church and cut him short. As the thunders died away, the voices of chanting priests ascended from the chancel, where some choir-boys were strewing rose-leaves over the marble steps leading to the altar. At the same moment the boom of a heavy gun, fired from the ramparts of the Castel dell' Ovo, shook the windows. The city ordnance was saluting St. Januarius — a custom that has since fallen into desuetude.

" Look ! " exclaimed Rose, laying her hand impulsively on Whitelaw's arm, " see the birds !   That's an exquisite fancy ! "

A flock of sparrows had been let loose, and were beating the misty air with uncertain wings, darting hither and thither through the nave and under the arches, in search of resting-places on frieze and cornice and jutting stonework. Meanwhile the priest had stepped down from the dais and was passing among the people, who crowded round him to press their lips and foreheads to the flask inclosed in the reliquary. The less devotional, and those who had already performed the rite, were slowly wending their way to the various outlets on the strada.

"I am glad it's over," declared White-law.

"To think," observed Rose reflectively, "that he has got to go all through it again to-morrow!"

"Who?"

"That poor dear saint."

"Oh," laughed Whitelaw, "I thought you meant me. *He* does n't mind it; it's his profession. There are objects more deserving of your pity. I, for instance, who have no sort of talent for martyrdom. You should have seen me — pinned to that column, like an entomological specimen, for forty mortal minutes! I would n't go through it again for a great deal."

"Not for the sake of meeting an old friend?"

"It was the old friend that made it particularly hard. To be so near her, and not able to speak to her! And part of the time not to have even the consolation of seeing the sweep of the ring-dove's wing on the left side of her new Paris hat."

Rose looked up into his face, and smiled

in a half absent way. She was far from
averse to having a detail of her toilet noticed by those she liked. In former days
Whitelaw had had a quick eye in such tri-
fles, and his remark seemed to her a verita-
ble little piece of the pleasant past, with an
odd, suggestive flavor about it.

She had slipped her hand through his
arm, and the pair were moving leisurely
with the stream towards one of the leather-
screened doors opening upon the vestibule.
The manner in which Rose fell in with
his step, and a certain subtile something
he recognized in the light pressure of her
weight, carried him, in his turn, very far
back into the olden time. The fifteen years,
like the two and thirty years in Tennyson's
lyric, were as a mist that rolls away. It
appeared to Whitelaw as if they had never
been separated, or had parted only yesterday. How naturally and sweetly she had
picked up the dropped thread of the old
friendship! The novelty of her presence
had evaporated at the first words she had
spoken; only the pleasure of it remained.

To him there was nothing strange or unexpected in their wholly unexpected and
entirely strange meeting. As he had told
her, he did not see how anything else could
have happened. Already he had acquired
the habit of being with her!

"Good heavens!" he said to himself, "it
can't be that I am falling in love with Rose
over again!"

The idea brought a flickering smile to
Whitelaw's lips, the idea of falling in love
at first sight — after a decennium and a
half!

"What are you smiling at?" she demanded, looking up alertly.

"I did n't know I was smiling."

"But you were; and an unexplained
smile when two persons are alone together,
with two thousand others, is as inadmissible
as whispering in company."

Whitelaw glanced at her with an amused,
partly embarrassed expression, and made
no response. They were passing at the instant through a narrow strip of daylight
slanted from one of the great blazoned

windows, and he was enabled to see Rose's
face with more distinctness than he hitherto
had done. If it had lost something of its
springtide bloom and outline — and he saw
that that was so — it had gained a beauty
of a rarer and richer sort. There was a
deeper lustre to the dark-fringed eyes, as if
they had learned to think, and a greater
tenderness in the curves of the mouth, as
if it had learned to be less imperious. How
handsome she was — handsomer than she
had been at nineteen !

In his rapid survey, Whitelaw's eye had
lighted on the small clasp holding the violets to her corsage — and rested there.
The faint flush that came to his cheek gradually deepened.

" Is that the clasp I gave you when you
were a girl ? " he finally asked.

" You recognize it ? — yes."

" And you 've kept the trifle all these
centuries ! "

" That 's not polite — when I was a girl,
several hundred years ago ! I kept it because it was a birthday gift ; because it

was a trifle ; then from habit, and now the centuries have turned it into a bit of price-less bric-à-brac."

Somehow Rose's explanation did not seem to him quite so exquisite as the bare fact itself.

Whitelaw was now conscious of a very perceptible acceleration in the flow of the current that was bearing them towards the cathedral entrance. It was not his purpose that they should reach it just yet. Their brief dialogue, carried on in undertone, and the early part of it with ecclesiastical in-terruptions, had been desultory and unsatis-fying. He should of course see much of Rose during her stay in Naples, for he had no intention of leaving it while she re-mained ; but the opportunity of having her to himself might not re-occur, and he had certain things to say to her which could not be said under any other condition. So many opportunities of various kinds had escaped him in the course of life that he resolved not to let this one slip. On the right of the eastern transept, he remembered, was a heavenly little chapel — the chapel of the Seripandis — where they might converse without restraint, if once they could get there.

Watching his chance, Whitelaw began a skillful oblique movement, and in a few minutes the two found themselves free of the crowd and in front of a gilded iron fencing, the gate of which stood open.

" This is not the way out ! " exclaimed Rose.

" I 'm aware of it," said Whitelaw.

" But we want to get out."

" You 've never visited the church before, have you, Rose ? "

" No."

" Then you ought to see some of the chapels. They contain things by Spagnoletto, Domenichino, and others. In this one, for instance, is an Assumption by Perugino. It would be a pity to miss that — now you are on the spot."

" I am afraid I have n't time for sight-seeing," she answered, drawing out a diminutive watch and pressing a spring in the stem. " I 've an engagement at ten " —

"Well, that leaves you more than half an hour," he interrupted, glancing over Rose's shoulder at the time-piece.

"But meanwhile Richard will be searching for me everywhere."

"Then he can't fail to find you here," said Whitelaw adroitly. "He has probably given you up, however, and gone back to the hotel."

"Perhaps he has," assented Rose irresolutely.

"In which case, I will take you home, or wherever you wish to be taken, when it is necessary for you to go."

"Oh, I'll not trouble you. The carriage was ordered to wait at the corner just below the church — the driver was not able to get nearer. That was to be our point of rendezvous. I don't know — perhaps I ought to go now."

Rose stood a second or two in an attitude of pretty hesitation, with her hand resting on one of the spear-heads of the gate ; then she stepped into the chapel.

IV

"It is not Perugino at his best," said Whitelaw, after a silence; "it has been restored in places, and not well done. I like some of his smaller canvases; but I don't greatly care for Perugino."

"Then why on earth have you dragged me in here to see it?" cried Rose.

"Because I care for you," he answered, smiling at the justice of her swift wrath. As he turned away from the painting, his countenance became grave.

"You have an original way of showing it. If I cared for any one, I would n't pick out objects of no interest for her to look at."

"Frankly, Rose, I was not willing to let you go so soon. I wanted a quiet half hour's talk with you. I had two or three serious things to say — things that have long been on my mind — and a chapel seemed the only fitting place to say them in."

This rather solemn exordium caused Rose to lift her eyelashes anxiously.

" I want, to speak of the past," said Whitelaw.

" No, do not let us speak of that," she protested hurriedly.

" After all this time, Rose, I think I have a kind of right " —

" No, you have no right whatever " —

— " to ask your forgiveness."

" My forgiveness — for what ? "

" For my long silence, and sullenness, and brutality generally. It was n't a crime in you not to love me in the old days, and I acted as if I regarded it as one. I was without any justification in going away from you in the mood I did that night."

" I was very, very sorry," said Rose gently.

" I should at once have accepted the situation, and remained your friend. That was a man's part, and I failed to play it. After a while, when I had recovered my reason, it was too late. It appears to be one of the conditions, if not the sole condition, of my existence that I should be too late. The occasion always slips away from me. When your — when I heard of Mr. Mason's death, if I had been another man I would have written to you, or sent you some sort of kindly message, for the old time's sake. The impulse to do so came to me three months afterwards. I sat down one day and began to write; then the futility and untimeliness of the whole thing struck me, and I tore up the letter."

"I wish you had not," said Rose. " A word from you then, or before Mr. Mason's death, would have been welcome to me. I was never willing to lose your friendship. After your first return from Europe, and you were seeing something of your own country, as every American ought to do, I hoped that you would visit San Francisco. I greatly desired that you should come and tell me, of your free will, that I was not to blame. If I had been, perhaps I would not have cared."

" You were blameless from beginning to end. I do not believe you ever said or did an insincere thing in your life, Rose. I simply misunderstood. The whole story lies in that. You were magnanimous to waste any thought whatever upon me. When I reflect on my own ungenerous attitude, I am ashamed to beg your pardon."

" I have not anything to forgive," Rose replied; and then she added, looking at him with a half rueful smile, " I suppose it was unavoidable, under the circumstances, that we should touch on this matter. Perhaps it was the only way to exorcise the ghost of the past; at all events, I am glad that you 've said what you have ; and now let it go. Tell me about yourself."

" I wish I could. There 's no more biography to me than if I were Shakespeare."

" What have you done all this while ? "

" Nothing."

" Where have you been ? "

" Everywhere."

" No pursuit, no study, no profession ? "

" Oh, yes ; I am a professional nomad —

an alien wherever I go. I'm an Englishman in America, and an American in England. They don't let up on me in either
country."

"Is n't there a kind of vanity in self-
disparagement, my friend? Seriously, if
you are not doing your own case injustice,
has n't this been a rather empty career? A
colonel at twenty-four — and nothing ever
after!"

"Precisely — just as if I had been killed
at Antietam." He wanted to say, "on
Beacon Hill."

"With your equipment, every path was
open to you. Most men have to earn their
daily bread with one hand, while they are
working for higher things with the other.
You had only the honors to struggle for.
To give up one's native land, and spend
years in aimless wandering from place to
place — it seems downright wicked."

"I've had some conscience in the matter," pleaded Whitelaw — "I might have
written books of travel and made a stock-
company of my *ennui*."

"You ought to have married, Marc," said Rose sententiously.

"I?" Whitelaw stared at her. How could Rose say a thing like that!

"Every man ought to marry," she supplemented.

"I admit the general proposition," he returned slowly, "but I object to the personal application. To the mass of mankind — meaning also womankind — marriage may be the only possible thing; but to the individual, it may be the one thing impossible. I would put the formula this way: Every one ought to wish to marry; some ought to be allowed to marry; and others ought to marry twice — to make the average good."

"That sounds Shakespearean — like your biography; but I don't think I have quite caught the idea."

"Perhaps it got tangled in the expression," said Whitelaw. "It was my purpose to pay a handsome tribute to matrimony, and to beg to be excused."

Rose remained silent a moment, with one

finger pressed against her cheek, making a little round white dent in it, and her eyes fixed upon the kneeling figure of Cardinal Carafa at the left of Perugino's picture. Then she turned, and fixed her eyes upon Whitelaw's figure.

"Have you never," she asked, "have you never, in all your journeyings, met a woman whom you liked?"

"I cannot answer you," he replied soberly, "without treading on forbidden ground. May I do that? When I first came abroad I fancy I rather hated women — that was one of the mild manifestations of my general insanity. Later, my hatred changed to morbid fastidiousness. My early education had spoiled me. I have, of course, met many admirable women, and admired them — at a safe distance."

"And thrown away your opportunities."

"But if I loved no one?"

"Admiration would have served."

"I do not agree with you, Rose."

"A man may do worse than make what the world calls a not wholly happy marriage."

Whitelaw glanced at her out of the corner of his eye. Was that an allusion to the late Richard Mason? The directness was characteristic of Rose; but the remark was a trifle too direct for *convenance*. If there were any esoteric intent in the words, her face did not betray it. But women can look less self-conscious than men.

" It seems to me," she went on, " that even an unromantic, commonplace union would have been better than the lonely, irresponsible life you have led, accepting your own statement of it — which I do not wholly. A man should have duties outside of himself; without them he is a mere balloon, inflated with thin egotism and drifting nowhere."

" I don't accept the balloon," protested Whitelaw, not taking kindly to Rose's metaphor. " That presupposes a certain internal specific buoyancy which I have not, if I ever had it. My type in the inanimate kingdom would be a diving-machine continually going down into wrecks in which there is apparently nothing to bring up. I would have it ultimately find the one precious ingot in the world."

"Oh, Marc," cried Rose earnestly, with just a diverting little touch of maternal solicitude in the gesture she made, "oh, Marc, I hope some day to see you happily married."

"You don't think it too late, then?"

"Too late? Why, you are only forty-three; and what if you were seventy-three? *On a l'âge de son cœur.*"

"Mine throws no light on the subject," said Whitelaw, with a thrill which he instantly repressed. "I suspect that my heart must be largely feminine, for it refuses to tell me its real age. At any rate, I do not trust it. Just now it is trying to pass itself off for twenty-five or thirty."

From time to time in the progress of this conversation a shadow, not attributable to any of the overhanging sculpture of the little Gothic chapel, had rested on Whitelaw's countenance. He had been assailed by strange surprises and conflicting doubts. Five or ten minutes before, the idea of

again falling in love with Rose had made
him smile. But was he not doing it, had he
not done it, or, rather, had he not always
loved her — more or less unconsciously?
And Rose? Her very candor perplexed
and baffled him, as formerly. She had always been a stout little Puritan, with her
sense of duty; but that did not adequately
explain the warmth with which she had
reproved him for his aimless way of life.
Why should his way of life so deeply concern her, unless . . . unless . . . In certain things she had said there had been a
significance that seemed perfectly clear to
him, though it had not lain upon the surface of the spoken words. Why had she
questioned him so inquisitorially? Why
had she desired to know if he had formed
any new lines of attachment? That indirect
reference to her own unfortunate marriage?
And then — though she explained it lightly
— had she not worn his boyish gift on her
bosom through all those years? The suggestion that they should return home on the
same steamer contained in itself a whole

little drama of likelihoods. What if destiny had brought him and Rose together at last! He did not dare think of it; he did not dare acknowledge to himself that he wished it, though he knew he did.

Whitelaw was now standing in the centre of the contracted apartment, a few feet from his companion, and looking at her meditatively. The cloud was gone from his brow, and a soft light had come into the clear gray eyes. Her phrase curled itself cunningly about his heart — *on a l'âge de son cœur!* He was afraid to speak again, lest an uncontrollable impulse should hurry him into speaking of his love; and that he felt would indeed be precipitate. But the silence which had followed his last remark was growing awkwardly long. He must break it with some platitude, if he could summon one.

"Now that my anatomization is ended," he said, tentatively, "is it not your turn, Rose? I have made a poor showing, as I warned you I should."

"My life has been fuller than yours,"

she returned, bending her eyes upon him
seriously, "and richer. I have had such
duties and pleasures as fall to most women,
and such sorrow as falls to many. . . . I
have lost a child."

The pathos of the simple words smote
Whitelaw to the heart.

"I — I had not heard," he faltered; and
a feeling of infinite tenderness for her came
over him. If he had dared he would have
gone to Rose and put his arm around her;
but he did not dare. He stood riveted to
the marble floor, gazing at her mutely.

"I did not mean to refer to that," she
said, looking up, with a lingering dimness
in the purple lashes. "No, don't let us
talk any more of the past. Speak to me of
something else, please."

"The future," said Whitelaw; "that can
give us no pain — until it comes, and is
gone. What are your plans for the summer?"

"We shall travel. I want Richard to
see as much as he can before he is tied
down to his studies, poor fellow!"

"Where do you intend to leave him at school?" inquired Whitelaw, with a quite recent interest in Richard.

"At Heidelberg or Leipsic — it is not decided."

"And meanwhile what's to be your route of travel?"

"We shall go to Sweden and Norway, and perhaps to Russia. I don't know why, but it has been one of the dreams of my life to see the great fair at Nijnii-Novgorod."

"It is worth seeing," said Whitelaw.

"It will be at its height in August — a convenient time for us. We could scarcely expect to reach St. Petersburg before August."

"I have just returned from Russia," he said, "after three years of it."

"Then you can give me some suggestions."

"Traveling there has numerous drawbacks unless one knows the language. French, which serves everywhere in Western Europe, is nearly useless in the majority of places. All educated Russians of course speak French or German; but railway-guards and drosky-drivers, and the persons with whom the mere tourist is brought most in contact, know only Russian."

"But we've an excellent courier," rejoined Rose, "who speaks all the tongues of Babel. His English is something superb."

"When do you start northward?" asked Whitelaw, turning on her quickly, with a sudden subtle prescience of defeated purpose.

"To-morrow."

"To-morrow!" he echoed, in consternation. "Then I am to see nothing of you!"

"If you've no engagement for to-night, come to the hotel. I should be very glad to " —

"Where are you staying?"

"At the United States, on the Chiatamone, like true patriots."

"I have no engagement," said Whitelaw bewilderedly.

Rose to leave Naples to-morrow! That was a death-blow to all his plans — the excursions in the environs, and all! She was slipping through his fingers again . . . he was losing her forever! There was no time for temporizing or hesitation. He must never speak, or speak now. Perhaps it would not seem abrupt or even strange to her. If so, Rose should remember that his position as a lover was exceptional — he had done his wooing fifteen years before! He confessed to himself — and he had often confessed it to that same severe critic of manners — that possibly his wooing had been somewhat lacking in dash and persistence then. But to-day he would win her, as he might perhaps have won her years ago, if he had not been infirm of purpose, or pigeon-livered, or too proud — which was it? He had let a single word repulse him, when the chances were he might have carried her by storm, or taken her by siege. How young he must have seemed, even in her young eyes! Now he had experience and knowledge of the world, and would not be denied. The doubts and misgivings that had clouded his mind for the last quarter of an hour were blown away like meadow-

mists at sunrise. At last he saw clearly.
He loved Rose — he had never really loved
her until this moment! For other men
there were other methods; there was but
one course for him. No; he would not go
to the hotel that night — as a suitor. His
fate should be sealed then and there in the
chapel of the Seripandis.

Whitelaw straightened himself, wavering
for an instant, like a foresail when it loses
the wind; then he crossed the narrow strip
of tessellated pavement that lay between
him and Rose, and stood directly in front
of her.

" Rose," he said, and there was a strange
pallor creeping into his cheeks, " there have
been two miracles wrought in this church
to-day. It is not only St. Januarius who
has, in a manner, come to life again. I,
too, have come to life. I have returned
once more to the world of living men and
women. Do not send me back! Let *me*
take you and your boy to Russia, Rose ! "

Rose gave a start, and cast a swift, hor-
rified look at Whitelaw's face.

"Marc!" she cried, convulsively grasping the wrist of the hand which he had held out to her, "is it possible you have n't heard — has no one told you — don't you *know* that I have married again " —

She stopped abruptly, and released his wrist.

A man in a frayed, well-brushed coat, with a courier's satchel depending from a strap over his shoulder, was standing outside the iron grille which separated the chapel from the main church.

"Madama," said the courier, as he respectfully approached through the gate, "it is ten o'clock. The Signor Schuyler and Master Richard are waiting with the carriage at the corner of the Strada dell' Antiogolia. They bade me inform Madama."

"FOR BRAVERY ON THE FIELD OF BATTLE"

I

THE recruiting-office at Rivermouth was in a small, unpainted, weather-stained building on Anchor Street, not far from the custom-house. The tumble-down shell had long remained tenantless, and now, with its mouse-colored exterior, easily lent itself to its present requirements as a little military mouse-trap. In former years it had been occupied as a thread-and-needle and candy shop by one Dame Trippew. All such petty shops in the town were always kept by old women, and these old women were always styled dames. It is to be lamented that they and their innocent traffic have vanished into the unknown.

The interior of the building, consisting

of one room and an attic covered by a lean-
to roof, had undergone no change beyond
the removal of Dame Trippew's pathetic
stock at the time of her bankruptcy. The
narrow counter, painted pea-green and di-
vided in the centre by a swinging gate, still
stretched from wall to wall at the further
end of the room, and behind the counter
rose a series of small wooden drawers, which
now held nothing but a fleeting and inac-
curate memory of the lavender, and penny-
royal, and the other sweet herbs that used
to be deposited in them. Even the tiny
cow-bell, which once served to warn Dame
Trippew of the advent of a customer, still
hung from a bit of curved iron on the inner
side of the street door, and continued to
give out a petulant, spasmodic jingle whenever that door was opened, however cautiously. If the good soul could have
returned to the scene of her terrestrial
commerce, she might have resumed business at the old stand without making any
alterations whatever. Everything remained
precisely as she had left it at the instant of

her exit. But a wide gulf separated Dame Trippew from the present occupant of the premises. Dame Trippew's slight figure, with its crisp, snowy cap and apron, and steel-bowed spectacles, had been replaced by the stalwart personage of a sergeant of artillery in the regular army, between whose overhanging red mustache and the faint white down that had of late years come to Dame Trippew's upper lip, it would have been impossible to establish a parallel. The only things these two might have claimed in common were a slackness of trade and a liking for the aromatic Virginia leaf, though Dame Trippew had taken hers in a dainty idealistic powder, and the sergeant took his in realistic plug through the medium of an aggressive clay pipe.

In spite of the starry shield, supported by two crossed cannon cut out of tin and surmounted by the national bird in the same material, which hung proudly over the transom outside ; in spite of the drum-mer-boy from the fort, who broke the si-lence into slivers at intervals throughout

the day; in brief, in spite of his own
martial bearing and smart uniform, the
sergeant found trade very slack. At Rivermouth the war with Mexico was not a
popular undertaking. If there were any
heroic blood left in the old town by the sea,
it appeared to be in no hurry to come forward and get itself shed. There were
hours in which Sergeant O'Neil despaired
of his country. But by degrees the situation brightened, recruits began to come in,
and finally the town and the outlying districts — chiefly the outlying districts —
managed to furnish a company for the
State regiment. One or two prominent
citizens had been lured by commissions as
officers; but neither of the two Rivermouthians who went in as privates was of
the slightest civic importance. One of
these men was named James Dutton.

Why on earth James Dutton wanted to
go to the war was a puzzle to the few towns-
folks who had any intimate acquaintance
with the young man. Intimate acquaintance is perhaps too strong a term; for

though Dutton was born in the town and
had always lived there, he was more or less
a stranger to those who knew him best.
Comrades he had, of course, in a manner:
the boys with whom he had formerly gone
to the public school, and two or three maturer persons whose acquaintance he had
contracted later in the way of trade. But
with these he could scarcely be said to be
intimate. James Dutton's rather isolated
condition was not in consequence of any
morbid or uncouth streak in his mental
make-up. He was of a shy and gentle
nature, and his sedentary occupation had
simply let the habit of solitude and un-
sociability form a shell about him. Dutton was a shoemaker and cobbler, like his
father before him; plying his craft in the
shabby cottage where he was born and had
lived ever since, at the foot of a narrow
lane leading down to the river — a lonely,
doleful sort of place, enlivened with a bit
of shelving sand where an ancient fisherman occasionally came to boil lobsters.

In the open lots facing the unhinged

gate was an old relinquished tannery that
still flavored the air with decayed hemlock
and fir bark, which lay here and there in
dull-red patches, killing the grass. The
undulations of a colonial graveyard broke
tamely against the western base of the
house. Headstones and monuments — if
there had ever been any monuments — had
melted away. Only tradition and those
slowly subsiding wave-like ridges of graves
revealed the character of the spot. Within
the memory of man nobody had been
dropped into that Dead Sea. The Dut-
tons, father and son, had dwelt here nearly
twenty-four years. They owned the shanty.
The old man was now dead, having laid
down his awl and lapstone just a year before the rise of those international compli-
cations which resulted in the appearance of
Sergeant O'Neil in Rivermouth, where he
immediately tacked up the blazoned ægis
of the United States over the doorway of
Dame Trippew's little shop.

As has been indicated, the war with
Mexico was not looked upon with favor by

the inhabitants of Rivermouth, who clearly
perceived its underlying motive — the extension of slave territory. The abolition
element in the town had instantly been
blown to a white heat. Moreover, war in
itself, excepting as a defensive measure or
on a point of honor, seemed rather poor
business to the thrifty Rivermouthians.
They were wholly of the opinion of Birdo-
fredom Sawin, that

" Nimepunce a day fer killin' folks comes kind o' low
fer murder."

That old Nehemiah Dutton's son should
have any interest one way or the other in
the questions involved was inconceivable,
and the morning he presented himself at
the recruiting-office a strong ripple of surprise ran over the group of idlers that hung
day after day around the door of the crazy
tenement, drawn thither by the drum-taps,
and a morbid sense of gunpowder in the
air. These idlers were too sharp or too un-
patriotic to enlist themselves, but they had
unbounded enthusiasm for those who did.
After a moment's hesitation, they cheered
Jemmy Dutton handsomely.

On the afternoon of his enlistment, he was met near the post-office by Marcellus Palfrey, the sexton of the Old Granite Church.

" What are you up to, anyhow, Jemmy?" asked Palfrey. " What 's your idee ? "

" My idea is," replied Dutton, " that I 've never been able to live freely and respectably, as I 've wanted to live; but I mean to die like a gentleman, when it comes to that."

" What do you call a gentleman, Jemmy ? "

" Well, a man who serves faithfully, and stands by to lay down his life for his duty — he 's a gentleman."

" That 's so," said Palfrey. " He need n't have no silver-plated handles, nor much outside finish, if he 's got a satin linin'. He 's one of God's men."

What really sent James Dutton to the war ? Had he some unformulated and hitherto unsuspected dream of military glory, or did he have an eye to supposable gold ingots piled up in the sub-basement of the halls of the Montezumas? Was it a case of despised love, or was he simply tired of reheeling and resoling the boots of Rivermouth folk; tired to death of the river that twice a day crept up to lap the strip of sandy beach at the foot of Nutter's Lane; tired to death of being alone, and poor, and aimless? His motive is not positively to be known, only to be guessed at. We shall not trouble ourselves about it. Neither shall the war, which for a moment casts a lurid light on his figure, delay us long. It was a tidy, comfortable little war, not without picturesque aspects. Out of its flame and smoke leaped two or three fine names that dazzled men's eyes awhile; and among the fortunate was a silent young lieutenant of infantry — a taciturn, but not unamiable young lieutenant — who was afterward destined to give the name of a great general into the keeping of history forever. Wrapped up somewhere in this Mexican war is the material for a brief American epic; but it is not to be unrolled and recited here.

WITH the departure of Our Country's Gallant Defenders, as they were loosely denominated by some — the Idiots, as they were compactly described by others — monotony again settled down upon Rivermouth. Sergeant O'Neil's heraldic emblems disappeared from Anchor Street, and the quick rattle of the tenor drum at five o'clock in the morning no longer disturbed the repose of peace-loving citizens. The tide of battle rolled afar, and its echoes were not of a quality to startle the drowsy old seaport. Indeed, it had little at stake. Only four men had gone from the town proper. One, Captain Kittery, died before reaching the seat of war; one deserted on the way; one, Lieutenant Bangs, was sent home invalided; and only James Dutton was left to represent the land force of his native town. He might as well have died or deserted, for he was promptly forgotten.

From time to time accounts of battles
and bombardments were given in the columns of " The Rivermouth Barnacle," on
which occasions the Stars and Stripes, held
in the claws of a spread eagle, decorated
the editorial page — a cut which until then
had been used only to celebrate the blood-
less victories of the ballot. The lists of
dead, wounded, and missing were always
read with interest or anxiety, as might happen, for one had friends and country acquaintance, if not fellow-townsmen, with
the army on the Rio Grande. Meanwhile
nobody took the trouble to bestow a thought
on James Dutton. He was as remote and
shadowy in men's memories as if he had
been killed at Thermopylæ or Bunker's
Hill. But one day the name of James Dutton blazed forth in a despatch that electri-
fied the community. At the storming of
Chapultepec, Private James Dutton, Company K, Rivermouth, had done a very
valorous deed. He had crawled back to
a plateau on the heights, from which the
American troops had been driven, and had

brought off his captain, who had been momentarily stunned by the wind of a round shot. Not content with that, Private Dutton had returned to the dangerous plateau, and, under a heavy fire, had secured a small field-piece which was about to fall into the hands of the enemy. Later in the day this little howitzer did eminent service. After touching on one or two other minor matters, the despatch remarked, incidentally, that Private James Dutton had had his left leg blown off.

The name of James Dutton was instantly on every lip in town. Citizens who had previously ignored his existence, or really had not been aware of it, were proud of him. The Hon. Jedd Deane said that he had long regarded James Dutton as a young man of great promise, a — er — most remarkable young person, in short; one of the kind with much — er — latent ability. Postmaster Mugridge observed, with the strong approval of those who heard him, that young Dutton was nobody's fool, though what especial wisdom Dutton had

evinced in having his leg blown off was not
clear. Captain Tewksberry, commanding
the local militia company, the Rivermouth
Tigers, was convinced that no one who had
not carefully studied "Scott's Tactics"
could have brought away that gun under
the circumstances. "Here, you will observe, was the exposed flank of the heights,
there, behind the *chevaux-de-frise*, lay the
enemy," etc., etc. Dutton's former school-
fellows began to remember that there had
always been something tough and gritty in
Jim Dutton. The event was one not to be
passed over by Parson Wibird Hawkins,
who made a most direct reference to it in
his Sunday's sermon — Job xxxix. 25 :
"He saith among the trumpets, Ha, ha;
and he smelleth the battle afar off, the
thunder of the captains, and the shouting."

After the first burst of local pride and
enthusiasm had exhausted itself over young
Dutton's brilliant action, the grim fact connected with young Dutton's left leg began
to occupy the public mind. The despatch
had vaguely hinted at amputation, and had

stopped there. If his leg had been shot away, was it necessary that the rest of him should be amputated? In the opinion of Schoolmaster Dennett, such treatment seemed almost tautological. However, all was presumably over by this time. Had poor Dutton died under the operation? Solicitude on that point was wide-spread and genuine. Later official intelligence relieved the stress of anxiety. Private Dutton had undergone the operation successfully and with great fortitude; he was doing well, and as soon as it was possible for him to bear transportation he was to be sent home. He had been complimented in the commanding officer's report of the action to headquarters, and General Winfield Scott had sent Private Dutton a silver medal "for bravery on the field of battle." If the Government had wanted one or two hundred volunteers from Rivermouth, that week was the week to get them.

Then intervened a long silence touching James Dutton. This meant feverish nights and weary days in hospital, and finally

blissful convalescence, when the scent of
the orange and magnolia blossoms blown in
at the open window seemed to James Dutton a richer recompense than he deserved
for his martyrdom.   At last he was in condition to be put on board a transport for
New Orleans.   Thence a man-of-war was to
convey him to Rivermouth, where the ship
was to be overhauled and have its own
wounds doctored.

When it was announced from the fort
that the vessel bearing James Dutton had
been sighted off the coast and would soon
be in the Narrows, the town was thrown
into such a glow of excitement as it had not
experienced since the day a breathless and
bedraggled man on horseback had dashed
into Rivermouth with the news that the
Sons of Liberty in Boston had pitched the
British tea overboard.   The hero of Chapultepec — the only hero Rivermouth had had
since the colonial period — was coming up
the Narrows!   It is odd that three fourths
of anything should be more estimable than
the whole, supposing the whole to be esti-

mable. When James Dutton had all his
limbs he was lightly esteemed, and here
was Rivermouth about to celebrate a fragment of him.

The normally quiet and unfrequented
street leading down to the boat-landing was
presently thronged by Rivermouthians —
men, women, and children. The arrival of
a United States vessel always stirred an
emotion in the town. Naval officers were
prime favorites in aristocratic circles, and
there were few ships in the service that did
not count among their blue-jackets one or
more men belonging to the port. Thus all
sea-worn mariners in Uncle Sam's employ
were sure of both patrician and democratic
welcome at Rivermouth. But the present
ship contained an especially valuable cargo.

It was a patient and characteristically
undemonstrative crowd that assembled on
the wharf, a crowd content to wait an hour
or more without a murmur after the ship
had dropped anchor in midstream for the
captain's gig to be lowered from the davits.
The shrill falsetto of the boatswain's whistle

suddenly informed those on shore of what was taking place on the starboard side, and in a few minutes the gig came sweeping across the blue water, with James Dutton seated in the stern-sheets and looking very pale. He sat there, from time to time pulling his blond mustache, evidently embarrassed. A cheer or two rose from the wharf when the eight gleaming blades simultaneously stood upright in air, as if the movement had been performed by some mechanism. The disembarkment followed in dead silence, for the interest was too novel and too intense to express itself noisily. Those nearest to James Dutton pressed forward to shake hands with him, but this ceremony had to be dispensed with as he hobbled on his crutches through the crowd, piloted by Postmaster Mugridge to the hack which stood in waiting at the head of the wharf.

Dutton was driven directly to his own little cottage in Nutter's Lane, which had been put in order for his occupancy. The small grocery closet had been filled with supplies, the fire had been lighted in the diminutive kitchen stove, and the tea-kettle was twittering on top, like a bird on a bough.   The Hawkins girls, Prudence and Mehitabel, had set some pansies and lilacs here and there in blue china mugs, and decorated with greenery the faded daguerreotype of old Nehemiah Dutton, which hung like a slowly dissolving ghost over his ancient shoemaker's bench.   As James Dutton hobbled into the contracted room where he had spent the tedious years of his youth and manhood, he had to lift a hand from one of the crutches to brush away the tears that blinded him.   It was so good to be at home again!

That afternoon, Dutton held an informal reception.   There was a constant coming and going of persons not in the habit of paying visits in so unfashionable a neighborhood as Nutter's Lane.   Now and then a townsman, conscious that his unimportance did not warrant his unintroduced presence inside, lounged carelessly by the door; and through the rest of the day several small boys turned somersaults and skylarked un-

der the window, or sat in rows on the rail-
fence opposite the gate. Among others
came the Hon. Jedd Deane, with his most
pronounced Websterian air — he was always
oscillating between the manner of Webster
and that of Rufus Choate — to pay his respects to James Dutton, which was considered a great compliment indeed. A few
days later, this statesman invited Dutton to
dine with him at the ancestral mansion in
Mulberry Avenue, in company with Parson
Wibird Hawkins, Postmaster Mugridge,
and Silas Trefethen, the Collector of the
Port. It was intimated that young Dutton
had handled himself under this ordeal with
as much self-possession and dignity as if he
had always dined off colonial china, and had
always stirred his after-dinner coffee with a
spoon manufactured by Paul Revere.

A motion to give James Dutton a limited
public banquet, at which the politicians
could have a chance to unfold their elo-
quence, was discussed and approved in the
Board of Selectmen, but subsequently laid
on the table, it being reported that Mr.

Dutton had declared that he would rather
have his other leg blown off than make a
speech. This necessarily killed the project,
for a reply from him to the chairman's
opening address was a *sine qua non*.

Life now opened up all sunshine to James
Dutton. His personal surroundings were of
the humblest, but it was home, sweet, sweet
home. One may roam amid palaces — even
amid the halls of the Montezumas — yet,
after all, one's own imperfect drain is the
best. The very leather-parings and bits of
thread that had drifted from the work-
bench into the front yard, and seemed to
have taken root there like some strange exotic weed, were a delight to him. Dutton's
inability to move about as in former years
sometimes irked him, but everything else
was pleasant. He resolved to make the best
of this one misfortune, since without it he
would never have been treated with such
kindness and consideration. The constant
employment he found at his trade helped
him to forget that he had not two legs. A
man who is obliged to occupy a cobbler's

bench day after day has no special need of
legs at all. Everybody brought jobs to his
door, and Dutton had as much work as he
could do. At times, indeed, he was forced
to decline a commission. He could hardly
credit his senses when this occurred.

So life ran very smoothly with him. For
the first time in his existence he found himself humming or whistling an accompani-
ment to the rat-tat-tat of his hammer on the
sole-leather. No hour of the twenty-four
hung heavily on him. In the rear of the
cottage was a bit of ground, perhaps forty
feet square, with an old elm in the centre,
under which Dutton liked to take his noon-
ing. It was here he used to play years ago,
a quiet, dreamy lad, with no companions
except the squirrels. A family of them still
inhabited the ancient boughs, and it amused
him to remember how he once believed that
the nimble brown creatures belonged to a
tribe of dwarf Indians who might attempt
to scalp him with their little knives if they
caught him out after dusk. Though his
childhood had not been happy, he had

reached a bend in the road where to pause and look back was to find the retrospect full of fairy lights and coloring.

Almost every evening one or two old acquaintances, with whom he had not been acquainted, dropped in to chat with him, mainly about the war. He had shared in all the skirmishes and battles from Cerro Gordo and Molino del Rey up to the capture of Chapultepec; and it was something to hear of these matters from one who had been a part of what he saw. It was considered a favor to be allowed to examine at short range that medal "for bravery on the field of battle." It was a kind of honor "just to heft it," as somebody said one night. There were visitors upon whom the impression was strong that General Scott had made the medal with his own hands.

James Dutton was ever modest in speaking of his single personal exploit. He guessed he did n't know what he was doing at the moment when he tumbled the howitzer into the ravine, from which the boys afterward fished it out. "You see, things

were anyway up on that plateau. The cop-
per bullets were flying like hailstones, so it
did n't much matter where a fellow went —
he was sure to get peppered. Of course
the captain could n't be left up there — we
wanted him for morning parades. Then
I happened to see the little field-piece
stranded among the chaparral. It was a
cursed nice little cannon. It would have
been a blighting shame to have lost it."

"I suppose you did n't leave your heart
down there along with the senoriteers, did
you, Jemmy?" inquired a town Lovelace.

"No," said Dutton, always perfectly matter of fact; "I left my leg."

Ah, yes; life was very pleasant to him in
those days!

Not only kindnesses, but honors were
showered upon him. Parson Wibird Hawkins, in the course of an address before the
Rivermouth Historical and Genealogical
Society, that winter, paid an eloquent tribute to "the glorious military career of our
young townsman" — which was no more
than justice; for if a man who has had a

limb shot off in battle has not had a touch of glory, then war is an imposition. Whenever a distinguished stranger visited the town, he was not let off without the question, " Are you aware, sir, that we have among us one of the heroes of the late Mexican war ? " And then a stroll about town to the various points of historic interest invariably ended at the unpretending door-step of Dutton's cottage.

At the celebration of the first Fourth of July following his return from Mexico, James Dutton was pretty nearly, if not quite, the chief feature of the procession, riding in an open barouche immediately behind that of the Governor. The boys would have marched him all by himself if it had been possible to form him into a hollow square. From this day James Dutton, in his faded coat and battered artillery cap, was held an indispensable adjunct to all turnouts of a warlike complexion. Nor was his fame wholly local. Now and then, as time went on, some old comrade of the Army of the Rio Grande, a member perhaps of old Company K, would turn up in Rivermouth for no other apparent purpose than to smoke a pipe or so with Dutton at his headquarters in Nutter's Lane. If he sometimes chanced to furnish the caller with a dollar or two of " the sinews of war," it was nobody's business. The days on which these visits fell were red-letter days to James Dutton.

It was a proud moment when he found himself one afternoon sitting, at School-master Dennett's invitation, on the platform in the recitation-room of the Temple Grammar School — sitting on the very platform with the green baize-covered table to which he had many a time marched up sideways to take a feruling. Something of the old awe and apprehension which Master Dennett used to inspire crept over him. There were instants when Dutton would have abjectly held out his hand if he had been told to do it. He had been invited to witness the evolutions of the graduating class in history and oratory, and the moisture gathered in his honest blue eyes when a panic-stricken urchin faltered forth —

" We were not many, we who stood
Before the iron sleet that day."

Dutton listened to it all with unruffled gravity. There was never a more gentle hero, or one with a slighter sense of humor, than the hero of Chapultepec.

Dutton's lot was now so prosperous as to exclude any disturbing thoughts concerning the future. The idea of applying for a pension never entered his head until the subject was suggested to him by Postmaster Mugridge, a more worldly man, an office-holder himself, with a carefully peeled eye on Government patronage. Dutton then reflected that perhaps a pension would be handy in his old age, when he could not expect to work steadily at his trade, even if he were able to work at all. He looked about for somebody to manage the affair for him. Lawyer Penhallow undertook the business with alacrity; but the alacrity was all on his side, for there were thousands of yards of red tape to be unrolled at Washington before anything in that sort could be done. At that conservative stage of our

national progress, it was not possible for a
man to obtain a pension simply because he
happened to know the brother of a man who
knew another man that had intended to go
to the war, and did n't. Dutton's claims,
too, were seriously complicated by the fact
that he had lost his discharge papers; so
the matter dragged, and was still dragging
when it ceased to be of any importance to
anybody.

Whenever James Dutton glanced into
the future, it was with a tranquil mind. He
pictured himself, should he not fall out of
the ranks, a white-haired, possibly a bald-
headed old boy, sitting of summer evenings
on the door-step of his shop, and telling
stories to the children — the children and
grandchildren of his present associates and
friends. He would naturally have laid up
something by that time; besides, there was
his pension. Meanwhile, though he moved
in a humble sphere, was not his lot an en-
viable one? There were long years of pleasant existence to be passed through before
he reached the period of old age. Of course

that would have its ailments and discom-
forts, but its compensations, also. It seemed
scarcely predictable that the years to come
held for him either great sorrows or great
felicities: he would never marry, and though
he might have to grieve over a fallen comrade here and there, his heart was not to be
wrung by the possible death of wife or child.
With the tints of the present he painted his
simple future, and was content.

Sometimes the experiences of the last few
years took on the semblance of a haunting
dream; those long marches through a land
rich with strange foliage and fruits, the en-
chanted Southern nights, the life in camp,
the roar of battle, and that one bewildering
day on the heights of Chapultepec — it all
seemed phantasmagoric. But there was his
mutilation to assure him of the reality, and
there on Anchor Street, growing grayer and
more wrinkled every season, stood the little
building where he had enlisted. To be sure,
the shield was gone from the transom, and
the spiders had stretched their reticulated
barricades across the entrance; but when-

ever Dutton hobbled by the place, he could
almost see Sergeant O'Neil leaning in an
insidious attitude against the door-sill, and
smoking his short clay pipe as of old. Yet
as time elapsed, this figure also grew indistinct and elusive, like the rest. Possibly —
but this is the merest conjecture, and has
bearing only on a later period — possibly
it may have sometimes occurred to James
Dutton, in a vague way, that after all there
had been something ironical and sinister in
his good fortune. The very circumstance
that had lifted him from his obscurity had
shut him out from further usefulness in life;
his one success had defeated him; he was
stranded, and could do no more. If such a
reflection ever came to him, no expression
of it found a way to his lips.

The weeks turned themselves into months,
and the months into years. Perhaps four
years had passed by when clouds of a perceptible density began to gather on James
Dutton's bright horizon.

The wisest of poets has told us that custom dulls the edge of appetite. One gets

used to everything, even to heroes.   James
Dutton was beginning to lose the bloom of
his novelty.   Indeed, he had already lost it.
The process had been so gradual, so subtile, in its working, that the final result
came upon him like something that had happened suddenly.   But this was not the fact.
He might have seen it coming, if he had
watched.   One by one his customers had
drifted away from him ; his shop was out
of the beaten track, and a fashionable boot
and shoe establishment, newly sprung up
in the business part of the town, had
quietly absorbed his patrons.   There was
no conscious unkindness in this desertion.
Thoughtless neglect, all the more bitter by
contrast, had followed thoughtless admiration.   Admiration and neglect are apt to
hunt in couples.   Nearly all the customers
left on Dutton's hands had resolved themselves into two collateral classes, those who
delayed and those who forgot to pay.   That
unreached pension, which flitted like an
ignis fatuus the instant one got anywhere
near it, would have been very handy to

have just then. The want of it had come
long before old age. Dutton was only
twenty-nine. Yet he somehow seemed old.
The indoor confinement explained his pallor,
but not the deepening lines that recently
began to spread themselves fan-like at the
corners of his eyes.

Callers at Nutter's Lane had now become
rare birds. The dwindling of his visitors
had at first scarcely attracted his notice;
it had been so gradual, like the rest. But
at last Dutton found himself alone. The
old solitude of his youth had re-knitted its
shell around him. Now that he was unsus-
tained by the likelihood of some one looking in on him, the evenings, especially the
winter evenings, were long to Dutton. Owing to weak eyes, he was unable to read
much, and then he was not naturally a
reader. He was too proud or too shy to
seek the companionship which he might
have found at Meeks's drug-store. Moreover, the society there was not of a kind
that pleased him; it had not pleased him in
the old days, and now he saw how narrow

and poor it was, having had a glimpse of
the broad world. The moonlight nights,
when he could sit at the window, and look
out on the gleaming river and the objects
on the further shore, were bearable. Something seemed always to be going on in the
old disused burying-ground; he was positive that on certain nights uncanny figures
flitted from dark to dark through a broad
intervening belt of silvery moonshine. A
busy spot after all these years ! But when
it was pitch-black outside, he had no resources. His work-bench with its polished
concave leather seat, the scanty furniture,
and his father's picture on the wall, grew
hateful to him. At an hour when the social life of the town was at its beginning,
he would extinguish his melancholy tallow-
dip and go to bed, lying awake until long
after all the rest of the world slumbered.
This lying awake soon became a habit. The
slightest sound broke his sleep — the gnaw-
ing of a mouse behind the mop-board, or
a change in the wind; and then insomnia
seized upon him. He lay there listening

to the summer breeze among the elms, or
to the autumn winds that, sweeping up
from the sea, teased his ear with muffled
accents of wrecked and drowning men.

The pay for the few jobs which came to
him at this juncture was insufficient to sup-
ply many of his simple wants. It was
sometimes a choice with him between food
and fuel. When he was younger, he used
to get all the chips and kindling he wanted
from Sherburn's shipyard, three quarters of
a mile away. But handicapped as he now
was, it was impossible for him to compass
that distance over the slippery sidewalk or
through the drifted road-bed. During the
particular winter here in question, James
Dutton was often cold, and oftener hungry
— and nobody suspected it.

A word in the ear of Parson Wibird
Hawkins, or the Hon. Jedd Deane, or any
of the scores of kind-hearted townsfolk,
would have changed the situation. But to
make known his distress, to appeal for
charity, to hold out his hand and be a
pauper — that was not in him. From his

point of view, if he could have done that,
he would not have been the man to rescue
his captain on the fiery plateau, and then
go back through that hell of musketry to
get the mountain howitzer.   He was se-
cretly and justly proud of saving his captain's life and of bringing off that " cursed
nice little cannon."   He gloried over it
many a time to himself, and often of late
took the medal of honor from its imitation-
morocco case, and read the inscription by
the light of his flickering candle.   The em-
bossed silver words seemed to spread a
lambent glow over all the squalid little
cabin — seemed almost to set it on fire !
More than once some irrepressible small boy,
prowling at night in the neighborhood and
drawn like a moth by the flame of Dutton's
candle, had set his eye to a crack in the
door-panel and seen the shoemaker sitting
on the edge of his bed with the medal in
his hand.

Until within a year or eighteen months,
Dutton had regularly attended the Sunday
morning service at the Old Granite Church.

One service was all he could manage, for it
was difficult for him to mount the steep
staircase leading to his seat in the gallery.
That his attendance slackened and finally
ceased altogether, he tried, in his own mind,
to attribute to this difficulty, and not to
the fact that his best suit had become
so threadbare as to make him ashamed;
though the congregation now seldom glanced
up, as it used to do, at the organ-loft where
he sat separated from the choir by a low
green curtain. Thus he had on his hands
the whole unemployed day, with no break
in its monotony; and it often seemed in-
terminable. The Puritan Sabbath as it
then existed was a thing not to be trifled
with. All temporal affairs were sternly set
aside; earth came to a standstill. Dutton,
however, conceived the plan of writing
down in a little blank-book the events of
his life. The task would occupy and divert
him, and be no flagrant sin. But there
had been no events in his life until the one
great event; so his autobiography resolved
itself into a single line on the first page —

Sept. 13, 1847.   Had my leg shot off.

What else was there to record, except a
transient gleam of sunshine immediately
after his return home, and his present help-
lessness and isolation ?

It was one morning at the close of a particularly bitter December.   The river-shore
was sheathed in thicker ice than had been
known for twenty years.   The cold snap,
with its freaks among water-pipes and win-
dow-glass and straw-bedded roots in front
gardens, was a thing that was to be remembered and commented on for twenty years
to come.   All natural phenomena have a
curious attraction for persons who live in
small towns and villages.   The weathercock
on the spire and the barometer on the back
piazza are studied as they are not studied
by dwellers in cities.   A habit of keen
observation of trivial matters becomes
second nature in rural places.   The pro-
vincial eye grows as sharp as the woods-
man's.   Thus it happened that somebody
passing casually through Nutter's Lane
that morning noticed — noticed it as a

thing of course, since it was so — that no
smoke was coming out of Dutton's chimney. The observer presently mentioned
the fact at the Brick Market up-town, and
some of the bystanders began wondering if
Dutton had overslept himself, or if he were
under the weather. Nobody recollected
seeing him lately, and nobody recollected
not seeing him ; a person so seldom in the
street as Dutton is not soon missed. Dr.
Meeks concluded that he would look in at
Nutter's Lane on the way home with his
marketing. The man who had remarked
the absence of smoke had now a blurred
impression that the shutters of Dutton's
shop-window had not been taken down.
It looked as if things were not quite right
with him. Two or three persons were going in Dr. Meeks's direction, so they accompanied him, and turned into Nutter's Lane
with the doctor.

The shop shutters were still up, and no
feather of smoke was curling from the one
chimney of Dutton's little house. Dr.
Meeks rapped smartly on the door without

bringing a response. After waiting a moment he knocked again, somewhat more heavily, but with like ill success. Then he tried the latch. The door was bolted.

" I think the lad must be sick," said Dr. Meeks, glancing hurriedly over his shoulder at his companions. " What shall we do ? "

" I guess we 'd better see if he is," said a man named Philbrick. " Let me come there," and without further words Philbrick pressed his full weight against the pine-wood panels. The rusty fastening gave way, and the door flew open. Cold as it was without, a colder breath seemed to issue from the interior. The door opened directly into the main apartment, which was Dutton's shop and sleeping-place in one. It was a lovely morning, and the sunshine, as if it had caught a glitter from the floating points of ice on the river, poured in through a rear window and flooded the room with gold. James Dutton was lying on his pallet in the further corner. He was dead. He must have been dead several hours, perhaps two or three days. The medal lay on his breast, from which his right hand had evidently slipped. The down-like frost on the medal was so thick as to make it impossible to distinguish the words —

"FOR BRAVERY ON THE FIELD OF BATTLE."

THE CHEVALIER DE RESSEGUIER

I

I AM unable to explain the impulse that prompted me to purchase it. I had no use for a skull — excepting, of course, the one I am temporarily occupying. There have been moments, indeed, when even that has seemed to me an incumbrance. Nevertheless, I bought another.

It was one of three specimens which decorated the window of a queer bookshop that I was in the habit of passing in my daily walks between the railway station and the office of the "Æsthetic Review." I was then living out of town. I call it a queer bookshop, for it was just that. It dealt in none but works on phrenology, toxicology, evolution, mesmerism, spiritualism, and kindred occult sciences. Against the door-

jambs, and on some shelves outside, were
piled small packages of quaintly bound volumes, each set tied up with a piece of frayed
twine, and bearing a tag on which was written the title of the work. These thin, dingy
octavos and twelvemos, looking as if they
might have come out of some mediæval
library, were chiefly treatises of a psychical
and social nature, and were no doubt dar-
ingly speculative. The patrons of the establishment shared its eccentricity. Now and
then I caught sight of a customer either
entering or leaving the shop. Sometimes
it was a half-shabby middle-aged man, who
seemed a cross between a low comedian
and a village undertaker; sometimes it was
a German or a Pole, cadaverous, heavy-
bearded, with a restlessness about the eyes
— a fellow that might be suspected of carry-
ing dynamite pellets in his waistcoat pocket;
and sometimes it was an elderly female,
severe of aspect, with short hair in dry
autumnal curls, evidently a person with ad-
vanced views on Man, and so flat in figure,
so wholly denuded of graceful feminine

curves, as to make it difficult for one to determine, when she lingered an instant in the doorway, whether she was going in or coming out.

What first attracted my attention to the shop-window was a plaster bust of the Young Augustus, for which a copy of Malthus on "The Principle of Population" served as pedestal. The cranium had been neatly marked out into irregular, variously colored sections, like a map of the United States. In each section was a Roman numeral, probably having its duplicate with an attendant explanation in the phrenological chart which lay in front of the bust. That first caught my eye; but the object which touched my real interest, and held it, was what I took to be a skillful imitation of the human skull, carved in rich old ivory. It struck me as a consummate little piece of sculpture, and I admired it greatly. After closer and repeated scrutiny, however, I discovered that it was not a reproduction, but the genuine article; yet I could never wholly divest myself of its first impression

as a work of art. A work of art, indeed!
It was one of a kind on which patient Nature has lavished some of her most exquisite
handicraft. What inanimate object on
earth so appeals to the imagination as a
skull, the deserted "dome of thought, the
palace of the soul," as Byron called it?
Reverently regarded, there is nothing de-
pressing or repellent in it. That is a false
and morbid sentimentalism which sees in
such relics anything but a solemn and
beautiful mystery.

There were, as I have said, two other
specimens in the window, but the one signal-
ized was incomparably the finest. I seldom
passed near the shop without halting a moment to contemplate the wide, placid brows,
in which there was a beauty of even a finer
kind than that in the face of the Young
Augustus, in spite of the latter having all
the advantage of completed features. The
skull was apparently very old — say a hundred years or so, if that is old for a skull;
and had clearly belonged to a man past the
prime of life at the instant of his quitting

it. It was a curious reflection that while time had ceased for the man himself, the inexorable years were surely, though slowly and imperceptibly, working their will on what was once so intimate a part of him, the cast-off shell of his mind!

Passing the shop day after day through those summer months, I finally became, if the phrase is permissible, on familiar terms with the skull. As I approached it morning and evening, on my passage to and fro, it grew to seem to me like the face of a friend in the crowd — a face that I should have missed if it had been absent. Once or twice as the declining sun chanced momentarily to light up the polished marble brows, I almost fancied that I detected a gleam of recognition on the part of the mask. It had such an air of shrewdness as it looked out on the busy life of the street! "What," I said to myself one evening — "what if by any possibility it has some dim perception of the fret and fever of it all — if some little flickering spark of consciousness still lingers!"

The idea, fanciful and illogical as it was, suggested itself to my mind from time to time, and one afternoon the pathos of it thrilled me strangely. I had a swift desire to take possession of the skull, and give it decent sepulture somewhere, though that would have been no kindly service if it were a sentient thing. At any rate, I resolved to shelter it from further publicity, and a moment afterward I found myself inside the old bookshop, and in close commercial relations with the proprietor, a moist-eyed but otherwise dessicated little man, whose *pince-nez*, attached by an elastic cord and set at an acute angle on his nose, was continually dropping into his shirt-bosom. There was something in the softness of his voice and the meekness of his manner out of all keeping with the revolutionary and explosive literature amid which he passed his existence.

" No," he said gently, in reply to a question I had put to him; " I cannot say whose it was. Of course," he added, with a feeble smile that had something of the pensiveness of a sigh, "it must have belonged to some one in particular; such things are not generally in common."

"I quite understand that," I returned. "I merely thought it might possibly have some sort of pedigree. Have you any idea how old it is?"

"There, too, I am in the dark," he replied deprecatingly. "It stood in the shop-window when I came here as a boy, somewhat more than fifty years ago. I distinctly remember upsetting it the very first morning I swept out the store. Where old Mr. Waldron got it — I succeeded to the business in 1859; will you let me give you one of my cards? — and how long he had had it in stock, I am unable to state. It is in perfect preservation, you will observe, and a gentleman wanting anything in this line, either for a collection or as a single specimen, could scarcely do better."

As the ancient bookseller spoke, he held out the skull on his palm at arm's length, and regarded it critically, giving a little purring hum of admiration meanwhile. I straightway thought of the grave-digger in the churchyard at Elsinore, and inwardly repeated Hamlet's comment: "Hath this fellow no feeling of his business, that he sings at grave-making?"

I was without definite views concerning the current prices of the merchandise I was about to purchase, but supposed that they ran rather high. I was astonished by the smallness of the sum named for the skull — a sum at which I should hesitate to part with my own, unless it were in some acute crisis of neuralgic headache.

The transaction concluded, I had an instant's embarrassment. "Could n't you wrap this in something?" I said.

"Certainly, to be sure!" exclaimed the little man, fishing up his eye-glasses for the twentieth time from the deep sea of his shirt-bosom. "Perhaps you would like it sent? If you will give me your address" —

"No, thanks. I live out of town. I will take it with me."

"Ah, quite so," he said, and, retiring to

an inner room, presently returned with the
skull neatly wrapped in a sheet or two of
pink tissue-paper.

I put it under my arm, and passed into
the street, trying to throw into my countenance the expression of a man who is carry-
ing home a melon. I succeeded so far in
this duplicity as to impose on my wife, who,
meeting me on the piazza of our little coun-
try-house, gayly snatched the package from
my hand, and remarked : —

" We will have it for dinner, dear ! "

We both were smiling as we entered the
house. In the mean while she was peeling
off the layers of tissue-paper.

" But it is n't a melon ! " cried my wife,
hastily laying the package on the hall table.

" No, dear," I said ; " it 's a skull."

" A skull ? How dreadful ! Where did
you get it ? Whose skull ? "

" It is mine — so far as such property
can be — for I bought it. It is more distinctly mine than the one I have, which I
did n't buy and pay for, but which was
thrown upon my hands, so to speak, without

any regard to my personal wishes in the matter. This one I wanted."

" But, my dear, what possessed you? It is perfectly horrid!"

" It is perfectly beautiful, my love, and it has the highest moral significance. It is probable that the original wearer of it conveyed no such deep lesson to his contemporaries as this surviving framework of him may have for us. The wise Athenians always had a skull at their banquets, to remind them of the transitoriness and vanity of life. So, after all, we can have it for dinner, dear. Gazing upon this symbol of impermanence, you will no longer envy Mrs. Midas her coupé, and I shall feel that old Midas's balance at the bank is not worth having, and that his ponderous new granite château, which completely cuts off our view of the river, is a thing of shifting sand. As a literary critic too much inclined, perhaps, to be severe on the shortcomings of fellow-creatures whose gifts are superior to mine, I need just such a *memento mori* to restrain my natural intolerance."

"How absurd! What do you mean to do with it?"

"I intend to put it on the faïence bracket over the end window in the library."

"Is it entirely appropriate as an ornament, dear? Is n't it a trifle — ghostly?"

"It is decidedly appropriate. What are books themselves but the lingering shades of dead and gone historians, story-tellers, and poets? Every library is full of ghosts, the air is thick with them."

"I am sure Jane will give us warning the moment she lays eyes on it."

"Then Jane can retire with her own silly head-piece."

"It will certainly terrify little Alfred."

"If it prevents little Alfred from playing in the library during my absence, and breaking the amber mouth-pieces off my best pipes, I shall not complain. But, seriously, I set a value on this ancient relic — a value which I cannot easily make clear even to myself. In speaking of the matter I have drifted into a lighter vein than I intended. The thing will not be out of place among the books and bric-à-brac in the library, where no one spends much time, excepting myself; so, like a good girl, say no more about it."

The question thus pleasantly settled itself. I had scarcely installed my singular acquisition on the bracket when I was called to dinner. I paused a moment or two with my hand on the knob of the library door to take in the general effect from that point of view. The skull, which in widely different surroundings had become a familiar object to me, adapted itself admirably to its new *milieu*. There was nothing incongruous or recent in its aspect; it seemed always to have stood just there, though the bracket had for years been occupied by a slender Venetian vase, a bit of Salviati's fragile workmanship, which only a few days previously had been blown from its stand by a draft caused by the sudden opening of the door.

" Yes," I said, " it will do very well. There 's nothing like it to give a tone to a library."

II

" WILL you take your coffee here, or have it in the library?" asked my wife, while Jane was removing the remains of the dessert.

" In the library," I said; "and as soon as Jane can fetch it. I must finish that review to-night."

When I bought the small house, half villa, half chalet, called Redroof, I added a two-story extension containing a spacious study on the ground-floor and a bedroom over it. As I frequently sat up late, and as Redroof was in a rather isolated situation, I liked to be within speaking-distance of my wife. By locking the doors of the upper and lower vestibules, which were connected by a staircase, we wholly separated ourselves from the main building. The library was a long low-studded apartment with three windows on each side, and at the

end opposite the door a wide-mullioned lat-
tice, with lead-set panes, overlooking a
stretch of lonely meadows. The quiet and
seclusion of the room made it an ideal spot
for literary undertakings, and here it was
that I did the greater part of my work.

Now I had an important piece of work
on hand this night, and after I had drunk
my coffee I began turning over the leaves
of a certain half-completed manuscript,
with the despairing consciousness that I
was not in a mood to go on with it. The
article in question was a study of political
intrigue during the reigns of Louis XV.
and Louis XVI. The subject had fasci-
nated me ; for a week I had been unable to
think of anything else, and the first part of
the article had almost written itself. But
now I found it impossible to pick up the
threads of my essay. My mind refused
concentration on any single point. A hundred things I wanted to say rushed upon
me simultaneously, and so jostled and ob-
scured one another as to create nothing but
confusion. This congestion of ideas is quite

as perplexing as their total absence, and the result is the same. I threw down my pen in disgust, and, placing one elbow on the desk, rested my cheek on my palm. I had remained in that attitude for perhaps three minutes when I heard a voice — a low but distinct voice — saying, —

" I beg monsieur's pardon, but if I interrupt him " —

I instantly wheeled round in my chair, expecting to see some one standing on the Bokhara rug behind me, though in the very act of turning I reflected how nearly impossible it was that any visitor could have got into the library at that time of night. There was nobody visible. I glanced toward the door leading into the vestibule. It was unlikely that that door could have been opened and closed without my observing it.

" I beg monsieur's pardon," repeated the voice, " but I am here — on the bracket."

" Oh," I said to myself, " I am careering round on the wildest of nightmares — one that has never before had a saddle on her.

Clearly this is the result of over-work."
My next impression was that I was being
made the victim of some ingenious practi-
cal joke. But no ; the voice had incontes-
tably issued from the little shelf above the
window, and though the effect might have
been accomplished by some acoustic con-
trivance, there was no one in the house or
in the neighborhood capable of conceiving
it. Since the thing was for the moment inexplicable, I decided to accept it on its own
terms. Recovering my composure, and fix-
ing my eyes steadily in the direction of the
bracket, I said : —

" Are you the person who just addressed
me ? "

" I am not a person, monsieur," replied
the voice slowly, as if with difficulty at
first, and with an unmistakable French ac-
cent ; " I am merely a conscience, an intelligence imprisoned in this sphere. Formerly
I was a person — a person of some slight
distinction, if I may be permitted so much
egotism. Possibly monsieur has heard of
me — I am the Chevalier de Resseguier."

Mechanically I threw a sheet of blotting-paper over the last page of my manuscript. Not five minutes previously I had written the following sentence — the ink was still fresh on the words : *Among the other intimates of Madame du Barry at this period was an adventurer from Toulouse, a pseudo man-of-letters, a sort of prowling epigram — one Chevalier* DE RESSEGUIER !

I had never been a believer in spiritualistic manifestations, perhaps for the simple reason that I had never been fortunate enough to witness any. Hitherto all phenomena had sedulously avoided me; but here was a mystery that demanded consideration — something that was not to be explained away on the theory that my senses had deceived me, something that the Society for Psychical Research would have been glad to get hold of. I found myself for once face to face with the Unusual, and I did not mean to allow it to daunt me. What is seemingly supernatural, is not always to be taken too seriously. The astrology of one age becomes the astronomy of the next; the magician disappears in the scientist. Perhaps it was an immense curiosity rather than any spirit of scientific investigation that gave steadiness to my nerves; for I was now as cool and collected as if a neighbor had dropped in to spend an hour with me. I placed the German student-lamp further back on the desk, crossed my legs, and settled myself comfortably in the chair, like a person disposed to be sociable.

" Did I understand you to say," I asked with deliberation, " that you were the Chevalier de Resseguier? "

" Yes, monsieur."

" The Chevalier de Resseguier whom Madame de Pompadour once sent to the Bastille for writing a certain vivacious quatrain? "

" Ah, monsieur knows me! I was certain of it! "

" The Chevalier de Resseguier who fluttered round the Du Barry at the time of her début, and later on figures in one or two chapters of her lively ' Mémoires '? "

"What! did the fair Jeannette give her 'Mémoires' to the world, and do I figure in them? Well, well! She had many talents, *la belle* Du Barry; she was of a cleverness! but I never suspected her of being a *bas bleu*. And so she wrote her 'Mémoires'!"

"Were you not aware of it?"

"Alas, monsieur, I know of nothing that has happened since that fatal July morning in '93 when M. Sanson — it was on the Place Louis Quinze — *chut!* and all was over."

"You mean you were" —

"Guillotined? *Certainement!* — thanks to M. Fouquier-Tinville. At that epoch everybody of any distinction passed through the hands of the *exécuteur des hautes œuvres* — a polite euphuism, monsieur. They were regenerating society in France by cutting off the only heads that had any brains in them. Ah, monsieur, though some few of us may not have known how to live, nearly all of us knew how to die!"

Though this De Resseguier had been in

his time a rascal of the first water — I had it down in black and white in my historical memoranda — there certainly was about him something of that chivalric dash, that ornateness of manner, that delightful in-souciance which we associate with the *XVIIIe siècle.* This air of high-breeding was no doubt specious, a thing picked up at the gateway of that gilded society which his birth and condition prevented him from entering. The De Choiseuls, the De Mau-peous, the D'Aiguillons — they were not for him. But he had breathed in a rich literary atmosphere, perhaps had spoken with Beaumarchais, or Rousseau, or Mar-montel, or Diderot — at least he had seen them. He had known his Paris well, that Paris which had a *mot* and a laugh on its lip until the glittering knife fell. He had witnessed the assembling of the Etats Gé-néraux ; had listened to Camille Desmoulins haranguing the populace from his green table in the garden of the Palais-Royal ; had gazed upon Citizen Marat lying in state at the Pantheon ; and had watched poor Louis Capet climb the scaffold stairs. Was he not " a mine of memories," this Chevalier de Resseguier ? If the chevalier had had a grain of honesty in him, I might have secured fresh and precious material for my essay — some unedited fact, some hitherto unused tint of local color; but I had his measure, and he was not to be trusted. So I attempted nothing of the sort, though the opportunity of interrogating him on certain points was alluring.

The silence which followed the chevalier's last remark was broken by myself.

" Chevalier," I said, " it is with great hesitation that I broach so delicate a matter, but your mention of M. Sanson recalls to my mind the controversy that raged among physiologists, at the close of the Reign of Terror, on a question similar to the one which is at this moment occupying our electricians. It was held by the eminent Dr. Süe that decapitation involved prolonged and exquisite suffering, while the equally eminent Dr. Sédillot contended that pain was simply impossible, an opinion which was sustained by the learned Gastellier. Will you, Chevalier, for the sake of science, pardon me if I ask you — was it quite painless? "

" M. le docteur Sédillot was correct, monsieur. Imagine a sensation a thousand times swifter than the swiftest thought, and monsieur has it."

" What followed then ? "

" Darkness and sleep."

" For how long, Chevalier ? "

" An hour — a month — a year — what know I ? "

" And then " —

" A glimmering light, consciousness, the past a vivid reality, the present almost a blur. *Voilà tout!* "

" In effect, Chevalier, you had left the world behind you, taking with you nothing but your personal memories — a light luggage, after all! As you are unfamiliar with everything that has occurred since that July morning, possibly it may interest you to learn that on December 7, 1793 — five months subsequent to your own departure

—the Comtesse du Barry was summoned before the Tribunal Révolutionnaire, and the next day " —

" She, too — *la pauvre petite!* I can fancy her not liking that at all."

" Indeed, Chevalier, the countess showed but faltering fortitude on this occasion. It is reported that she cried, ' Grâce, monsieur le bourreau; encore un moment!' It was not for such as she to mount the scaffold with the tread of a Charlotte Corday."

" *Ma foi, non!* She was a frank *coquine*, when truth is said. But who is all bad? She was not treacherous like Félicité de Nesle, nor vindictive like the Duchesse de Châteauroux. There was not a spark of malice in her, monsieur. When it was easy for her to do so, the Du Barry never employed against her enemies — and she had many — those *lettres de cachet* which used to fly in flocks, like blackbirds, from the hand of Madame de Pompadour."

" It is creditable to your heart, Chevalier — or, rather, to your head — that you have a kindly word for Madame du Barry."

" To be sure she thrust her adorable arm up to the elbow in the treasure-chest of Louis *le bien-aimé,* but then she was generous. She patronized art — and sometimes literature. The painter and the sculptor did not go unpaid — *elle donnait à deux mains.* Possibly monsieur has seen Pajou's bust of her? *Quel chef-d'œuvre!* And that portrait by Drouais — *le joli museau!*"

" I have seen the bust," I replied, glad to escape into the rarefied atmosphere of the arts; " it is in the Louvre at present, and, as you observe, a masterpiece. The Drouais portrait has not fallen in my way. There 's an engraving of it, I believe, in one of Paul de Saint-Victor's interesting volumes. Ah, yes, I forgot; he is not of your world. But how is it, Chevalier, that with your remarkable conversational power " —

" Monsieur is too flattering."

" How is it that you have not informed yourself concerning the progress of human events, and especially of the political, literary, and social changes that have taken place in France? Surely you have had opportunities rarely offered, I imagine, to one in your position. Now, at the bookshop where I — where I made your acquaintance, you might have interrogated many intelligent persons."

" Ah, that miserable *boutique!* and that superannuated vender of revolutionary pamphlets — an imbecile of imbeciles, monsieur! How could I have talked with him and his fellow *crétins*, even if it had been possible! But it was not possible. Monsieur is the only person to whom I have ever been able to communicate myself. A barrier of dense materialism has until now excluded me from such intercourse as monsieur suggests. I make my compliments to monsieur; he is *tout à fait spirituel!* "

" May I inquire, Chevalier," I said, after a moment of meditation, " if the mind, the vital spark, of all persons who pass through a certain inevitable experience takes final lodgment in the cranium? I begin then to comprehend why that part of the anatomy of man has been rendered almost indestructible."

"I am grieved that I cannot dispel the darkness enveloping monsieur's problem. Perhaps this disposition of the vital spark, as monsieur calls it, occurs only in the case of those persons who have made their exit under peculiar circumstances. I cannot say. Chance has doubtless brought me in contact with several persons of that class, but no sign of recognition has passed between us. As I understand it, monsieur, death is a transition state, like life itself, and leaves the mystery still unsolved. Outside of my own individual consciousness everything has been nearly a blank."

"Then, possibly, you don't know where you are at present?"

"I conjecture; I am far from positive, but I think I am in the land of Benjamin Franklin."

"Well, yes; but I should say the late Benjamin Franklin, if I were you. It is many years since he was an active factor in our public affairs."

"I was not aware — my almost absolute seclusion — monsieur understands."

" In your retirement, Chevalier, you have missed much. Vast organic upheavals have occurred meanwhile; things that seemed to reach down to the bed-rock of permanence have been torn up by the roots. The impossible has become the commonplace. The whole surface of the earth has undergone a change, and nowhere have the changes been more radical and marvelous than in your own beloved France. Would you not like me briefly to indicate a few of them?"

" If monsieur will be so obliging."

" In the first place, you should know that Danton, Desmoulins, Robespierre, and the rest, each in his turn, fell into the hands of your old friend M. Sanson."

" *A la bonne heure!* I knew it would come to that. When France wanted to regenerate society she ought to have begun with the *sans culottes*."

" The republic shortly gave way to a monarchy. A great soldier sat upon the throne, a new Cæsar, who flung down his gauntlet to the whole world, and well-nigh conquered it; but he too fell from his lofty height, suddenly, like Lucifer, never to rise again."

" And how did men call him ? "

" Napoleon Bonaparte."

" Bonaparte ? Bonaparte ? — it is not a French name, monsieur."

" After him the Bourbon reigned ; then there was a republic ; and then another Cæsar came — an imitation Cæsar — who let a German king conquer France, and bivouac his Uhlans under the lime-trees in the Champs Elysées."

" A German with his foot upon the neck of France ! Ah, monsieur, was I not happy to escape the knowledge of all these things? *Mon Dieu!* but he was a prophet, that Louis XV., with his ' Après nous le déluge ! ' Tell me no more ! I am well content to wait in ignorance."

" To wait for what, Chevalier ? "

" For the end of the world, I suppose. Really, monsieur puts the most perplexing questions — like a *juge d'instruction.*"

I may here remark that throughout our conversation the immobility of the face of the Chevalier de Resseguier, taken in connection with what he was saying, had a grotesque effect. His moods were many, but his expression was one. Whether he spoke sadly, or playfully, or vehemently, there was that stolid, stony outline, gazing into vacancy like the face of a sphinx.

" But, Chevalier," I said, "it must be a monotonous business, this waiting."

" Yes, and no, monsieur. I am at least spared the tumult and struggle of earthly existence; for what is the life of man but *une milice continuelle?* Here I am safe from debts and the want of *louis d'or* to pay them ; safe from false love, false friendship, and all hypocrisy. I am neither hot nor cold, neither hungry nor thirsty. *Parbleu!* monsieur, I might be much worse off."

" Yet at intervals your solitude must weigh upon you."

" Then I take a little nap of four or five years — four or five years according to monsieur's computation. The Gregorian calendar does not exist for me."

"Perhaps you feel like taking a little nap now," I suggested, with a sudden desire to be rid of him.

"Not at all," replied the chevalier briskly. "I never felt less like it."

"I am sorry, for it is really an embarrassing question, when I come to think of it, what I am to do with you."

"Monsieur is too kind to trouble himself with thinking about it. Why do anything? How charming it all has been, except that Madame for an instant mistook me for a melon! We have our little vanities, *nous autres!* Here I find myself *au mieux*. I am a man of letters, a poet whose works have been crowned by the Bastille if not by the Académie. These volumes in polished calf and fragrant crushed levant make a congenial atmosphere, *n'est-ce pas?* Formerly my Greek and Latin were not of the best; but now, naturally, I speak both with fluency, for they are *dead* languages, as monsieur is aware. My English — monsieur can judge. I acquired it in London during a year or two when my presence in Paris was not absolutely indispensable. So why not let me remain where I am? *Un bel esprit* is never *de trop*. Monsieur need never more be in want of a pleasant companion. I will converse with him, I will dissipate his *ennui*. I am no longer of those who disappear abruptly. I will stay with monsieur forever."

This monstrous proposition struck me cold.

" No, Chevalier," I said, with as much calmness as I could command; " such an arrangement would not suit me in any particular. You have not read the ' Mémoires ' of Madame du Barry, and I have. Our views of life are antagonistic. The association you propose is wholly impracticable."

" I am here by monsieur's own invitation, am I not? Did I thrust myself upon him? No. Did I even seek his acquaintance? No. It was monsieur who made all the advances. There were three of us, and he selected me. I am deeply sensible of the honor. I would give expression to that sensibility. I would, if monsieur were disposed, render him important literary services. For example, I could furnish him with many curious particulars touching the Œil-de-Bœuf, together with some startling facts which establish beyond doubt the identity of the Man in the Iron Mask."

" Such information, unfortunately, would be of no use to me."

" Of no use ? Monsieur astonishes me ! "

" I could not avail myself of statements made by the Chevalier de Resseguier."

" Monsieur means " —

" Precisely what I say."

" But what monsieur says is not precisely clear. His words are capable of being construed as insulting. Under different circumstances, I should send two of my friends to demand of monsieur the satisfaction which one *galant homme* never refuses another."

" And you would get it ! " I returned warmly.

" I could wish that I had monsieur for one little quarter of an hour in some shady avenue at Versailles, or on the Terrasse des Feuillants in the garden of the Tuileries."

" I wish you had, and then you 'd wish you had n't, for I should give you a sound caning to add to your stock of permanent reminiscences."

" Monsieur forgets himself," said the chevalier, and the chevalier was quite right. " The rapier and the pistol are — or were — my weapons. Fortunately for monsieur I am obliged to say *were*. Monsieur can be impertinent with impunity."

" I 've a great mind to knock your head off ! " I cried, again in the wrong.

" A work of supererogation. I beg leave to call monsieur's unintelligent attention to the fact that my head is already off."

" It 's a pity," I said, " that persons of your stripe cannot be guillotined two or three times. However, I can throw you out of the window."

" Throw me out of the window ! " cried the Chevalier de Resseguier in a rage.

At that instant the door of the library was opened hurriedly, and a draft of wind, sweeping through the apartment, tumbled the insecurely placed skull from its perch.

"Do you know how late it is, dear?" said my wife, standing on the threshold, with a lace shawl drawn about her shoulders and her bare feet thrust into a pair of Turkish slippers. "It is half past two. I verily believe you must have fallen asleep over your work!"

I stared for a moment at my wife, and made no reply. Then I picked up the Chevalier de Resseguier, who had sustained a double fracture of the jaw, and carefully replaced him, fragments and all, on the little faïence bracket over the window.

GOLIATH

It was raining — softly, fluently, persistently — raining as it rains on the afternoon of the morning when you hesitate a minute or two at the hat-stand, and finally decide not to take your umbrella down town with you. It was one of those fine rains — I am not praising it — which wet you to the skin in about four seconds. A sharp twenty-minutes' walk lay between my office in Court Street and my rooms in Huntington Avenue. I was standing meditatively in the doorway of the former establishment on the lookout for a hack or a herdic. An unusual number of these vehicles were hurrying in all directions, but as each approached within the arc of my observation the face of some fortunate occupant was visible through the blurred glass of the closed window.

Presently a coupé leisurely turned the corner, as if in search of a fare. I hailed the driver, and though he apparently took no notice of my gesture, the coupé slowed up and stopped, or nearly stopped, at the curbstone directly in front of me. I dashed across the narrow sidewalk, pulled open the door, and stepped into the vehicle. As I did so, some one else on the opposite side performed the same evolution, and the two of us stood for an instant with the crowns of our hats glued together. Then we seated ourselves simultaneously, each by this token claiming the priority of possession.

"I beg your pardon, sir," I said, "but this is my carriage."

"I beg *your* pardon, sir," was the equally frigid reply; "the carriage is mine."

"I hailed the man from that doorway," I said, with firmness.

"And I hailed him from the crossing."

"But I signaled him first."

My companion disdained to respond to that statement, but settled himself back on the cushions as if he had resolved to spend the rest of his life there,

" We will leave it to the driver," I said.

The subject of this colloquy now twisted his body round on the dripping box, and shouted : —

" Where to, gentlemen ? "

I lowered the plate glass, and addressed him : —

" There 's a mistake here. This gentleman and I both claim the coupé. Which of us first called you ? " But the driver " could n't tell t' other from which," as he expressed it. Having *two* fares inside, he of course had no wild desire to pronounce a decision that would necessarily cancel one of them.

The situation had reached this awkward phase when the intruder leaned forward and inquired, with a total change in his intonation : —

" Are you not Mr. David Willis ? "

" That is my name."

" I am Edwin Watson ; we used to know each other slightly at college."

All along there had been something familiar to me in the man's face, but I had

attributed it to the fact that I hated him
enough at first sight to have known him
intimately for ten years. Of course, after
this, there was no further dispute about the
carriage. Mr. Watson wanted to go to the
Providence station, which lay directly on
the route to Huntington Avenue, and I was
charmed to have his company. We fell
into pleasant chat concerning the old Har-
vard days, and were surprised when the
coupé drew up in front of the red-brick
clock-tower of the station.

The acquaintance, thus renewed by
chance, continued. Though we had resided
six years in the same city, and had not met
before, we were now continually meeting —
at the club, at the down-town restaurant
where we lunched, at various houses where
we visited in common. Mr. Watson was in
the banking business; he had been married
one or two years, and was living out of
town, in what he called "a little box," on
the slope of Blue Hill. He had once or
twice invited me to run out to dine and
spend the night with him, but some engage-

ment or other disability had interfered.
One evening, however, as we were playing
billiards at the St. Botolph, I accepted his
invitation for a certain Tuesday.   Watson,
who was having a vacation at the time, was
not to accompany me from town, but was to
meet me with his pony-cart at Green Lodge,
a small flag-station on the Providence railway, two or three miles from "The Briers,"
the name of his place.

"I shall be proud to show you my wife,"
he said, " and the baby — and Goliath."

" Goliath ? "

" That 's the dog," answered Watson,
with a laugh.   " You and Goliath ought to
meet — David and Goliath ! "

If Watson had mentioned the dog earlier
in the conversation I might have shied at
his hospitality.   I may as well at once confess that I do not like dogs, and am afraid
of them.   Of some things I am not afraid ;
there have been occasions when my courage
was not to be doubted — for example, the
night I secured the burglar in my dining-
room, and held him until the police came ;

and notably the day I had an interview with a young bull in the middle of a pasture, where there was not so much as a burdock leaf to fly to; with my red-silk pocket-handkerchief I deployed him as coolly as if I had been a professional *matador*. I state these unadorned facts in no vainglorious mood. If that burglar had been a collie, or that bull a bull-terrier, I should have collapsed on the spot.

No man can be expected to be a hero in all directions. Doubtless Achilles himself had his secret little cowardice, if truth were known. That acknowledged vulnerable heel of his was perhaps not his only weak point. While I am thus covertly drawing a comparison between myself and Achilles, I will say that that same extreme sensitiveness of heel is also unhappily mine; for nothing so sends a chill into it, and thence along my vertebræ, as to have a strange dog come up sniffing behind me. Some inscrutable instinct has advised all strange dogs of my antipathy and pusillanimity.

> "The little dogs and all,
> Tray, Blanche, and Sweetheart, see, they bark at me."

They sally forth from picturesque verandas and unsuspected hidings, to show their teeth as I go by. In a spot where there is no dog, one will germinate if he happens to find out that I am to pass that way. Sometimes they follow me for miles. Strange dogs that wag their tails at other persons growl at me from over fences, and across vacant lots, and at street corners.

"So you keep a dog?" I remarked carelessly, as I dropped the spot-ball into a pocket.

"Yes," returned Watson. "What is a country-place without a dog?"

I said to myself, "I know what a country-place is *with* a dog; it's a place I should prefer to avoid."

But as I had accepted the invitation, and as Watson was to pick me up at Green Lodge station, and, presumably, see me safely into the house, I said no more.

Living as he did on a lonely road, and likely at any hour of the night to have a burglar or two drop in on him, it was proper that Watson should have a dog on

the grounds. In any event he would have
done so, for he had always had a maniacal
passion for the canine race. I remember
his keeping at Cambridge a bull-pup that
was the terror of the neighborhood. He
had his rooms outside the college-yard in
order that he might reside with this fiend.
A good mastiff or a good collie — if there
are any good collies and good mastiffs —
is perhaps a necessity to exposed country-
houses; but what is the use of allowing him
to lie around loose on the landscape, as is
generally done? He ought to be chained
up until midnight. He should be taught to
distinguish between a burglar and an in-
offensive person passing along the highway
with no intention of taking anything but
the air. Men with a taste for dogs owe it
to society not to cultivate dogs that have an
indiscriminate taste for men.

The Tuesday on which I was to pass the
night with Watson was a day simply packed
with evil omens. The feathered cream at
breakfast struck the key-note of the day's
irritations. Everything went at cross-pur-

poses in the office, and at the last moment a telegram imperatively demanding an answer nearly caused me to miss that six o'clock train — the only train that stopped at Green Lodge. There were two or three thousand other trains which did not stop there. I was in no frame of mind for rural pleasures when I finally seated myself in the " six o'clock accommodation " with my gripsack beside me.

The run from town to Green Lodge is about twenty-five minutes, and the last stoppage before reaching that station is at Readville. We were possibly half-way between these two points when the train slackened and came to a dead halt amid some ragged woodland. Heads were instantly thrust out of the windows right and left, and everybody's face was an interrogation. Presently a brakeman, with a small red flag in his hand, stationed himself some two hundred yards in the rear of the train, in order to prevent the evening express from telescoping us. Then our engine sullenly detached itself from the tender, and disappeared. What had happened? An overturned gravel-car lay across the track a quarter of a mile beyond. It was fully an hour before the obstruction was removed, and our engine had backed down again to its coupling. I smiled bitterly, thinking of Watson and his dinner.

The station at Green Lodge consists of a low platform upon which is a shed covered on three sides with unpainted deal boards hacked nearly to pieces by tramps. In autumn and winter the wind here, sweeping across the wide Neponset marshes, must be cruel. That is probably why the tramps have destroyed their only decent shelter between Readville and Canton. On this evening in early June, as I stepped upon the platform, the air was merely a ripple and a murmur among the maples and willows.

I looked around for Watson and the pony-cart. What had occurred was obvious. He had waited an hour for me, and then driven home with the conviction that the train must have passed before he got there, and that I, for some reason, had failed to come on it. The capsized gravel-car was an episode of which he could have known nothing.

A walk of three miles was not an inspiriting prospect, and would not have been even if I had had some slight idea of where " The Briers " was, or where I was myself. At one side of the shed, and crossing the track at right angles, ran a straight, narrow road that quickly lost itself in an arbor of swamp-willows. Beyond the tree-tops rose the serrated line of the Blue Hills, now touched with the twilight's tenderest amethyst. Over there, in that direction somewhere, lay Watson's domicile.

" What I ought to have done to-day," I reflected, " was to stay in bed. This is one of the days when I am unfitted to move among my fellow-men, and cope with the complexities of existence."

Just then my ear caught the sound of a cart-wheel grating on an unoiled axle. It was a withered farmer in a rickety open wagon slowly approaching the railway track, and going toward the hills — my own intended destination. I stopped the man and explained my dilemma. He was willing, after a suspicious inventory of my person, to give me a lift to the end of the Green Lodge road. There I could take the old turnpike. He believed that the Watson place was half a mile or so down the turnpike toward Milton way. I climbed up beside him with alacrity.

Beyond giving vent to a sneeze or two left over from the previous winter, the old man made no sign of life as we drove along. He seemed to be in a state of suspended animation. I was as little disposed to talk.

It was a balmy evening, the air was charged with sweet wood-scents, and here and there a star half-opened an eyelid on the peaceful dusk. After the frets of the day, it was soothing thus to be drawn at a snail's pace through the fragrance and stillness of that fern-fringed road, with the night weaving and unweaving its mysteries of light and shade on either side. Now and then the twitter of an oriole in some pendent nest overhead added, as it were, to the silence. I was yielding myself up wholly to the glamour of the time and place, when suddenly I thought of Goliath. At that moment Goliath was probably prowling about Watson's front yard seeking whom he might devour; and I was that predestined nourishment.

I knew what sort of watch-dog Watson would be likely to keep. There was a tough streak in Watson himself, a kind of thoroughbred obstinacy — the way he had held on to that coupé months before illustrated it. An animal with a tenacious grip, and on the verge of hydrophobia, was what would naturally commend itself to his liking. He had specified Goliath, but maybe he had half a dozen other dragons to guard his hillside Hesperides. I had depended on Watson meeting me at the station, and now, when I was no longer expected, I was forced to invade his premises in the darkness of the night, and run the risk of being torn limb from limb before I could make myself known to the family. I recalled

Watson's inane remark, " You and Goliath ought to meet — David and Goliath ! " It now struck me as a most unseemly and heartless pleasantry.

These reflections were not calculated to heighten my enjoyment of the beauties of nature. The gathering darkness, with its few large, liquid stars, which a moment before had seemed so poetical, began to fill me with apprehension. In the daylight one has resources, but what on earth was I going to do in the dark with Goliath, and, likely enough, a couple of bloodhounds at my throat? I wished myself safely back among the crowded streets and electric lights of the city. In a few minutes more I was to be left alone and defenseless on a dismal highway.

When we reached the junction of the Green Lodge road and the turnpike, I felt that I was parting from the only friend I had in the world. The man had not spoken two words during the drive, and now rather gruffly refused my proffered half-dollar ; but I would have gone home with him if he had asked me. I hinted that it would be much to his pecuniary advantage if he were willing to go so far out of his course as the door-step of Mr. Watson's house; but either because wealth had no charms for him, or because he had failed to understand my proposition, he made no answer, and, giving his mare a slap with the ends of the reins, rattled off into space.

On turning into the main road I left behind me a cluster of twinkling lights emitted from some dozen or twenty little cottages, which, as I have since been told, constitute the village of Ponkapog. It was apparently alive with dogs. I heard them going off, one after another, like a string of Chinese crackers, as the ancient farmer with his creaking axle passed on through the village. I was not reluctant to leave so alert a neighborhood, whatever destiny awaited me beyond.

Fifteen or twenty minutes later I stood in front of what I knew at a glance to be "The Briers," for Watson had described it to me. The three sharp gables of his description had not quite melted into the blackness which was rapidly absorbing every object; and there too, but indistinct, were the twin stone gate-posts with the cheerful Grecian vases on top, like the entrance to a cemetery.

I cautiously approached the paling and looked over into the inclosure. It was gloomy with shrubbery, dwarf spruces, and Norway pines, and needed nothing but a few obelisks and lachrymal urns to complete the illusion. In the centre of the space rose a circular mound of several yards in diameter, piled with rocks, on which probably were mosses and nasturtiums. It was too dark to distinguish anything clearly; even the white gravel walk encircling the mound left one in doubt. The house stood well back on a slight elevation, with two or three steps leading down from the piazza to this walk. Here and there a strong light illumined a lattice-window. I particularly noticed one on the ground floor in an ell of the building, a wide window with diamond-shaped panes — the dining-room. The curtains were looped back, and I could see the pretty housemaid in her cap coming and going. She was removing the dinner things: she must have long ago taken away *my* unused plate.

The contrast between a brilliantly lighted, luxurious interior and the bleak night outside is a contrast that never appeals to me in vain. I seldom have any sympathy for the outcast in sentimental fiction until the inevitable moment when the author plants her against the area-railing under the windows of the paternal mansion. I like to have this happen on an inclement Christmas or Thanksgiving eve — and it always does.

But even on a pleasant evening in early June it is not agreeable to find one's self excluded from the family circle, especially when one has traveled fifteen miles to get there. I regarded the inviting façade of Watson's villa, and then I contemplated the sombre and unexplored tract of land which I must needs traverse in order to reach the door-step. How still it was!

The very stillness had a sort of menace in it. My imagination peopled those black interstices under the trees with "gorgons and hydras and chimæras dire." There certainly was an air of latent dog about the place, though as yet no dog had developed. However, unless I desired to rouse the inmates from their beds, I saw that I ought to announce myself without much further delay. I softly opened the gate, which, having a heavy ball-and-chain attachment, immediately slipped from my hand and slammed to with a bang as I stepped within.

I was not surprised, but I was paralyzed all the same, at instantly hearing the familiar sound of a watch-dog suddenly rushing from his kennel. The kennel in this instance was on a piazza: a convenient arrangement — for the dog — in case of visitors.

The next sound I heard was the scrabble of the animal's four paws as he landed on the graveled pathway. There he hesitated, irresolute, as if he were making up his diabolical mind which side of the mound he would take. He neither growled nor barked in the interim, being evidently one of those wide-mouthed, reticent brutes that mean business and indulge in no vain flourish. I afterward changed my mind on the latter point.

I held my breath, and waited. Presently I heard him stealthily approaching me on the left. I at once hastened up the right-hand path, having tossed my gripsack in his direction, with the hope that while he was engaged in tearing it to pieces, I might possibly be able to reach the piazza and ring the door-bell.

My ruse failed, however, and the gripsack, which might have served as a weapon of defense, had been sacrificed. The dog continued his systematic approach, and I was obliged to hurry past the piazza-steps. A few seconds brought me back to the point of my departure. Superficially considered, the garden-gate, which now lay at my hand, offered a facile mode of escape; but I was ignorant of the fastenings; I had forgotten which way it swung; besides, as I had no stop-over ticket, it was necessary that I should continue on my circular journey.

So far as I could judge, the dog was now about three yards in my rear; I was unable to see him, but I could plainly detect his quick respiration, and his deliberate foot-falls on the gravel. I wondered why he did not spring upon me at once; but he knew he had his prey, he knew I was afraid of him, and he was playing with me as a cat plays with a mouse. In certain animals there is a refinement of cruelty which some-times makes them seem almost human. If I believed in the transmigration of souls, I should say that the spirit of Caligula had passed into dogs, and that of Cleopatra into cats.

It is easily conceivable that I made no such reflection at the moment, for by this time my brisk trot had turned into a run, and I was spinning around the circle at the rate of ten miles an hour, with the dog at my heels. Now I shot by the piazza, and now past the gate, until presently I ceased to know which was the gate and which the piazza. I believe that I shouted "Watson!" once or twice, no doubt at the wrong place, but I do not remember. At all events, I failed to make myself heard. My brain was in such confusion that at intervals I could not for the soul of me tell whether I was chasing the dog, or the dog was chasing me. Now I almost felt his nose at my heel, and now I seemed upon the point of trampling him underfoot.

My swift rotatory movement, combined with the dinner which I had not had, soon induced a sort of vertigo. It was a purely unreasoning instinct that prevented me from flying off at a tangent and plunging into the shrubbery. Strange lights began to come into my eyes, and in one of those phosphorescent gleams I saw a shapeless black object lying, or crouching, in my path. I automatically kicked it into the outer darkness. It was only my derby hat, which had fallen off on one of the previous trips.

I have spoken of the confused state of

my mind. The right lobe of my brain had
suspended all natural action, but with the
other lobe I was enabled to speculate on the
probable duration of my present career. In
spite of my terror, an ironical smile crept to
my lips as I reflected that I might perhaps
keep this thing up until sunrise, unless a
midnight meal was one of the dog's regular
habits. A prolonged angry snarl now and
then admonished me that his patience was
about exhausted.

I had accomplished the circuit of the
mound for the tenth — possibly the twentieth — time (I cannot be positive), when the
front door of the villa was opened with a
jerk, and Watson, closely followed by the
pretty housemaid, stepped out upon the
piazza. He held in his hand a German
student-lamp, which he came within an ace
of dropping as the light fell upon my countenance.

"Good heavens! Willis; is this you?
Where did you tumble from? What's become of your hat? How did you get *here?*"

"Six o'clock train — Green Lodge —
white horse — old man — I"—

Suddenly the pretty housemaid descended the steps and picked up from the graveled path a little panting, tremulous wad of something — not more than two handfuls at most — which she folded tenderly to her bosom.

" What 's that ? " I asked.

" That 's Goliath," said Watson.

MY COUSIN THE COLONEL

I

Mrs. Wesley frequently embarrasses me by remarking in the presence of other persons — our intimate friends, of course — "Wesley, you are not brilliant, but you are good."

From Mrs. Wesley's outlook, which is that of a very high ideal, there is nothing uncomplimentary in the remark, nothing so intended, but I must confess that I have sometimes felt as if I were paying a rather large price for character. Yet when I reflect on my cousin the colonel, and my own action in the matter, I am ready with gratitude to accept Mrs. Wesley's estimate of me, for if I am not good, I am not anything. Perhaps it is an instance of my lack of brilliancy that I am willing to relate certain facts which strongly tend to substantiate this.   My purpose, however, is not to prove either my goodness or my dullness, but to leave some record, even if slight and imperfect, of my only relative.   When a family is reduced like ours to a single relative, it is well to make the most of him. One should celebrate him annually, as it were.

One morning in the latter part of May, a few weeks after the close of the war of the rebellion, as I was hurrying down Sixth Avenue in pursuit of a heedless horse-car, I ran against a young person whose shabbiness of aspect was all that impressed itself upon me in the instant of collision.   At a second glance I saw that this person was clad in the uniform of a Confederate soldier — an officer's uniform originally, for there were signs that certain insignia of rank had been removed from the cuffs and collar of the thread-bare coat.   He wore a wide-brimmed felt hat of a military fashion, decorated with a tarnished gilt cord, the two ends of which, terminating in acorns, hung down over his nose. His butternut trousers were tucked into the tops of a pair of high cavalry boots, of such primitive workmanship as to suggest the possibility that the wearer had made them himself. In fact, his whole appearance had an impromptu air about it. The young man eyed me gloomily for half a minute; then a light came into his countenance.

" Wesley — Tom Wesley ! " he exclaimed. " Dear old boy ! "

To be sure I was Thomas Wesley, and, under conceivable circumstances, dear old boy; but who on earth was he?

" You don't know me ? " he said, laying a hand on each of my shoulders, and leaning back as he contemplated me with a large smile in anticipatory enjoyment of my surprise and pleasure when I should come to know him. " I am George W. Flagg, and long may I wave ! "

My cousin Flagg ! It was no wonder that I did not recognize him.

When the Flagg family, consisting of

father and son, removed to the South,
George was ten years old and I was thirteen. It was twenty years since he and I
had passed a few weeks together on Grandfather Wesley's farm in New Jersey. Our
intimacy began and ended there, for it had
not ripened into letters; perhaps because
we were too young when we parted. Later
I had had a hundred intermittent impulses
to write to him, but did not. Meanwhile
separation and silence had clothed him in
my mind with something of the mistiness of
a half-remembered dream. Yet the instant
Washington Flagg mentioned his name,
the boyish features began rapidly to define
themselves behind the maturer mask, until
he stood before me in the crude form in
which my memory had slyly embalmed him.

Now my sense of kinship is particularly
strong, for reasons which I shall presently
touch upon, and I straightway grasped my
cousin's hand with a warmth that would
have seemed exaggerated to a bystander,
if there had been a bystander; but it was
early in the day, and the avenue had not

yet awakened to life.   As this bitter world goes, a sleek, prosperous, well-dressed man does not usually throw much heartiness into his manner when he is accosted on the street by so unpromising and dismal an object as my cousin Washington Flagg was that morning.   Not at all in the way of sounding the trumpet of my own geniality, but simply as the statement of a fact, I will say that I threw a great deal of heartiness into my greeting.   This man to me meant Family.

I stood curiously alone in the world. My father died before I was born, and my mother shortly afterwards.   I had neither brother nor sister.   Indeed, I never had any near relatives except a grandfather until my sons came along.   Mrs. Wesley, when I married her, was not merely an only child, but an orphan.   Fate denied me even a mother-in-law.   I had one uncle and one cousin.   The former I do not remember ever to have seen, and my association with the latter, as has been stated, was of a most limited order.   Perhaps I should have had less sentiment about family ties if I had had more of them. As it was, Washington Flagg occupied the position of sole kinsman, always excepting the little Wesleys, and I was as glad to see him that May morning in his poverty as if he had come to me loaded with the title-deeds of those vast estates which our ancestors (I wonder that I was allowed any ancestors: why was n't I created at once out of some stray scrap of protoplasm?) were supposed to have held in the colonial period. As I gazed upon Washington Flagg I thrilled with the sense that I was gazing upon the materialization in a concrete form of all the ghostly brothers and sisters and nephews and nieces which I had never had.

"Dear old boy!" I exclaimed, in my turn, holding on to his hand as if I were afraid that I was going to lose him again for another twenty years. "Bless my stars! where did you come from?"

"From Dixie's Land," he said, with a laugh. "'Way down in Dixie."

In a few words, and with a picturesqueness of phrase in which I noted a rich Southern flavor, he explained the phenomenon of his presence in New York. After Lee's surrender at Appomattox Court House, my cousin had managed to reach Washington, where he was fortunate enough to get a free pass to Baltimore. He had nearly starved to death in making his way out of Virginia. To quote his words, "The wind that is supposed to be tempered expressly for shorn lambs was not blowing very heavily about that time." At Baltimore he fell in with a former Mobile acquaintance, from whom he borrowed a sum sufficient to pay the fare to New York — a humiliating necessity, as my cousin remarked, for a man who had been a colonel in Stonewall Jackson's brigade. Flagg had reached the city before daybreak, and had wandered for hours along the water-front, waiting for some place to open, in order that he might look up my address in the Directory, if I were still in the land of the living. He had had what he described as an antediluvian sandwich the previous day at two o'clock, since which banquet no food had passed his lips.

"And I'll be hanged," he said, "if the first shop that took down its shutters was n't a restaurant, with a cursed rib of roast beef, flanked with celery, and a ham in curl-papers staring at me through the window-pane. A little tin sign, with 'Meals at All Hours' painted on it — what did they want to go and do that for? — knocked the breath clean out of me. I gave one look, and ploughed up the street, for if I had stayed fifteen seconds longer in front of that plate-glass, I reckon I would have burst it in. Well, I put distance between me and temptation, and by and by I came to a newspaper office, where I cornered a Directory. I was on the way to your house when we collided; and now, Tom Wesley, for heaven's sake introduce me to something to eat. There is no false pride about me; I'd shake hands with a bone."

The moisture was ready to gather in my eyes, and for a second or two I was unable to manage my voice. Here was my only kinsman on the verge of collapse — one miserable sandwich, like a thin plank, between him and destruction. My own plenteous though hasty morning meal turned into reproachful lead within me.

"Dear old boy!" I cried again. "Come along! I can see that you are nearly famished."

"I've a right smart appetite, Thomas, there's no mistake about that. If appetite were assets, I could invite a whole regiment to rations."

I had thrust my hand under his arm, and was dragging him towards a small oyster shop, whose red balloon in a side street had caught my eye, when I suddenly remembered that it was imperative on me to be at the office at eight o'clock that morning, in order to prepare certain papers wanted by the president of the board, previous to a meeting of the directors. (I was at that time under-secretary of the Savonarola Fire Insurance Company.) The recollection of the business which had caused me to be on foot at this unusual hour brought me to a dead halt. I dropped my cousin's arm, and stood looking at him helplessly. It seemed so inhospitable, not to say cold-blooded, to send him off to get his breakfast alone. Flagg misinterpreted my embarrassment.

" Of course," he said, with a touch of dignity which pierced me through the bosom, " I do not wish to be taken to any place where I would disgrace you. I know how impossible I am. Yet this suit of clothes cost me twelve hundred dollars in Confederate scrip. These boots are not much to look at, but they were made by a scion of one of the first families of the South; I paid him two hundred dollars for them, and he was right glad to get it. To such miserable straits have Southern gentlemen been reduced by the vandals of the North. Perhaps you don't like the Confederate gray?"

" Bother your boots and your clothes!" I cried. " Nobody will notice them here." (Which was true enough, for in those days the land was strewed with shreds and patches of the war. The drivers and conductors of street cars wore overcoats made out of shoddy army blankets, and the dustmen went about in cast-off infantry caps.) "What troubles me is that I can't wait to start you on your breakfast."

"I reckon I don't need much starting."

I explained the situation to him, and suggested that instead of going to the restaurant, he should go directly to my house, and be served by Mrs. Wesley, to whom I would write a line on a leaf of my memorandum-book. I did not suggest this step in the first instance because the little oyster saloon, close at hand, had seemed to offer the shortest cut to my cousin's relief.

"So you 're married?" said he.

"Yes — and you?"

"I have n't taken any matrimony in mine."

"I 've been married six years, and have two boys."

"No! How far is your house?" he inquired. "Will I have to take a caar?"

"A 'caar'? Ah, yes — that is to say, no. A car is n't worth while. You see that

bakery two blocks from here, at the right?
That's on the corner of Clinton Place.
You turn down there. You'll notice in
looking over what I've written to Mrs.
Wesley that she is to furnish you with
some clothes, such as are worn by — by
vandals of the North in comfortable circumstances."

"Tom Wesley, you are as good as a
straight flush. If you ever come down
South, when this cruel war is over, our people will treat you like one of the crowned
heads — only a devilish sight better, for the
crowned heads rather went back on us. If
England had recognized the Southern Con-
federacy " —

"Never mind that; your tenderloin steak
is cooling."

"Don't mention it! I go. But I say,
Tom — Mrs. Wesley? Really, I am
hardly presentable. Are there other ladies
around?"

"There's no one but Mrs. Wesley."

"Do you think I can count on her being
glad to see me at such short notice?"

"She will be a sister to you," I said warmly.

"Well, I reckon that you two are a pair of trumps. *Au revoir!* Be good to yourself."

With this, my cousin strode off, tucking my note to Mrs. Wesley inside the leather belt buckled tightly around his waist. I lingered a moment on the curbstone, and looked after him with a sensation of mingled pride, amusement, and curiosity. That was my Family; there it was, in that broad back and those not ungraceful legs, striding up Sixth Avenue, with its noble intellect intent on thoughts of breakfast. I was thankful that it had not been written in the book of fate that this limb of the closely pruned Wesley tree should be lopped off by the sword of war. But as Washington Flagg turned into Clinton Place, I had a misgiving. It was hardly to be expected that a person of his temperament, fresh from a four years' desperate struggle and a disastrous defeat, would refrain from expressing his views on the subject. That those views would be somewhat lurid, I was convinced by the phrases which he had dropped here and there in the course of our conversation. He was, to all intents and purposes, a Southerner. He had been a colonel in Stonewall Jackson's brigade. And Mrs. Wesley was such an uncompromising patriot ! It was in the blood. Her great-grandfather, on the mother's side, had frozen to death at Valley Forge in the winter of 1778, and her grandfather, on the paternal side, had had his head taken off by a round-shot from his Majesty's sloop of war Porpoise in 1812. I believe that Mrs. Wesley would have applied for a divorce from me if I had not served a year in the army at the beginning of the war.

I began bitterly to regret that I had been obliged to present my cousin to her so abruptly. I wished it had occurred to me to give him a word or two of caution, or that I had had sense enough to adhere to my first plan of letting him feed himself at the little oyster establishment round the corner. But wishes and regrets could not now mend the matter; so I hailed an approaching horse-car, and comforted myself on the rear platform with the reflection that perhaps the colonel would not wave the palmetto leaf too vigorously, if he waved it at all, in the face of Mrs. Wesley.

II

THE awkwardness of the situation disturbed me more or less during the forenoon ; but fortunately it was a half-holiday, and I was able to leave the office shortly after one o'clock.

I do not know how I came to work myself into such a state of mind on the way up town, but as I stepped from the horse-car and turned into Clinton Place I had a strong apprehension that I should find some unpleasant change in the facial aspect of the little red brick building I occupied — a scowl, for instance, on the brown-stone eye-brow over the front door. I actually had a feeling of relief when I saw that the façade presented its usual unaggressive appearance.

As I entered the hall, Mrs. Wesley, who had heard my pass-key grating in the lock, was coming downstairs.

" Is my cousin here, Clara ? " I asked,

in the act of reaching up to hang my hat on the rack.

" No," said Mrs. Wesley. There was a tone in that monosyllable that struck me.

" But he has been here ? "

" He has been here," replied Mrs. Wesley. " Maybe you noticed the bell-knob hanging out one or two inches. Is Mr. Flagg in the habit of stretching the bell-wire of the houses he visits, when the door is not opened in a moment ? Has he escaped from somewhere ? "

" ' Escaped from somewhere ! ' " I echoed.

" I only asked ; he behaved so strangely."

" Good heavens, Clara ! what has the man done ? I hope that nothing unpleasant has happened. Flagg is my only surviving relative — I may say *our* only surviving relative — and I should be pained to have any misunderstanding. I want you to like him."

" There was a slight misunderstanding at first," said Clara, and a smile flitted across her face, softening the features which had worn an air of unusual seriousness and preoccupation. "But it is all right now, dear. He has eaten everything in the house, the bit of spring lamb I saved expressly for you ; and has gone down town 'on a raid,' as he called it, in your second-best suit — the checked tweed. I did all I could for him."

"My dear, something has ruffled you. What is it ? "

"Wesley," said my wife slowly, and in a perplexed way, "I have had so few relatives that perhaps I don't know what to do with them, or what to say to them."

"You always say and do what is just right."

"I began unfortunately with Mr. Flagg, then. Mary was washing the dishes when he rang, and I went to the door. If he *is* our cousin, I must say that he cut a remarkable figure on the door-step."

"I can imagine it, my dear, coming upon you so unexpectedly. There *were* peculiarities in his costume."

"For an instant," Clara went on, "I took him for the ashman, though the ashman always goes to the area door, and never comes on Tuesdays; and then, before the creature had a chance to speak, I said, ' We don't want any,' supposing he had something to sell. Instead of going away quietly, as I expected him to do, the man made a motion to come in, and I slammed the door on him."

" Dear ! dear ! "

" What else could I do, all alone in the hall ? How was I to know that he was one of the family ? "

" What happened next ? "

" Well, I saw that I had shut the lapel of his coat in the door-jamb, and that the man could n't go away if he wanted to ever so much. Was n't it dreadful ? Of course I did n't dare to open the door, and there he was ! He began pounding on the panels and ringing the bell in a manner to curdle one's blood. He rang the bell at least a hundred times in succession. I stood there with my hand on the bolt, not daring to move or breathe. I called to Mary to put on her things, steal out the lower way, and bring the police. Suddenly everything was still outside, and presently I saw a piece of paper slowly slipping in over the threshold, oh, so slyly! I felt my hands and feet grow cold. I felt that the man himself was about to follow that narrow strip of paper; that he was bound to get in that way, or through the key-hole, or somehow. Then I recognized your handwriting. My first thought was that you had been killed in some horrible accident " —

" And had dropped you a line ? "

" I didn't reason about it, Wesley ; I was paralyzed. I picked up the paper, and read it, and opened the door, and Mr. Flagg rushed in as if he had been shot out of something. ' Don't want any ? ' he shouted. ' But I do ! I want some breakfast ! ' You should have heard him."

" He stated a fact, at any rate. Of course he might have stated it less vivaciously." I was beginning to be amused.

" After that he was quieter, and tried to make himself agreeable, and we laughed a little together over my mistake — that is, *he* laughed. Of course I got breakfast for him — and such a breakfast!"

"He had been without anything to eat since yesterday."

"I should have imagined," said Clara, "that he had eaten nothing since the war broke out."

"Did he say anything in particular about himself?" I asked, with a recurrent touch of anxiety.

"He wasn't particular what he said about himself. Without in the least seeing the horror of it, he positively boasted of having been in the rebel army."

"Yes — a colonel."

"That makes it all the worse," replied Clara.

"But they had to have colonels, you know."

"Is Mr. Flagg a Virginian, or a Mississippian, or a Georgian?"

"No, my dear; he was born in the State of Maine; but he has lived so long in the South that he's quite one of them for the present.   We must make allowances for him, Clara.   Did he say anything else?"

"Oh yes."

"What did he say?"

"He said he'd come back to supper."

It was clear that Clara was not favorably impressed by my cousin, and, indeed, the circumstances attending his advent were not happy.   It was likewise clear that I had him on my hands, temporarily at least. I almost reproach myself even now for saying "on my hands," in connection with my own flesh and blood.   The responsibility did not so define itself at the time.   It took the form of a novel and pleasing duty. Here was my only kinsman, in a strange city, without friends, money, or hopeful outlook.   My course lay before me as straight as a turnpike.   I had a great deal of family pride, even if I did not have any family to speak of, and I was resolved that what little I had should not perish for want of proper sustenance.

Shortly before six o'clock Washington Flagg again presented himself at our door-

step, and obtained admission to the house
with fewer difficulties than he had encoun-
tered earlier in the day.

I do not think I ever saw a man in des-
titute circumstances so entirely cheerful as
my cousin was. Neither the immediate
past, which must have been full of hard-
ships, nor the immediate future, which was
not lavish of its promises, seemed to give
him any but a momentary and impersonal
concern. At the supper table he talked
much and well, exceedingly well, I thought,
except when he touched on the war, which
he was continually doing, and then I was
on tenter-hooks. His point of view was so
opposed to ours as to threaten in several instances to bring on an engagement all along
the line. This calamity was averted by my
passing something to him at the critical
moment. Now I checked his advance by a
slice of cold tongue, and now I turned his
flank with another cup of tea; but I questioned my ability to preserve peace throughout the evening. Before the meal was at
an end there had crept into Clara's manner

a polite calmness which I never like to see.
What was I going to do with these two
after supper, when my cousin Flagg, with
his mind undistracted by relays of cream
toast, could give his entire attention to the
Lost Cause?

As we were pushing the chairs back from
the table, I was inspired with the idea of
taking our guest off to a café concert over
in the Bowery — a *volksgarten* very popular
in those days.   While my whispered suggestion was meeting Clara's cordial approval, our friend Bleeker dropped in.   So
the colonel and Bleeker and I passed the
evening with "lager-beer and Meyerbeer,"
as my lively kinsman put it; after which he
spent the night on the sofa in our sitting-
room, for we had no spare chamber to place
at his disposal.

"I shall be very snug here," he said,
smiling down my apologies.   "I'm a 'possum for adapting myself to any odd hollow."

The next morning my cousin was early
astir, possibly not having found that narrow

springless lounge all a 'possum could wish, and joined us in discussing a plan which I had proposed overnight to Mrs. Wesley, namely, that he should hire an apartment in a quiet street near by, and take his meals — that was to say, his dinner — with us, until he could make such arrangements as would allow him to live more conveniently. To return South, where all the lines of his previous business connections were presumably broken, was at present out of the question.

"The war has ruined our people," said the colonel. "I will have to put up for a while with a place in a bank or an insurance office, or something in that small way. The world owes me a living, North or South."

His remark nettled me a little, though he was, of course, unaware of my relations with the Savonarola Fire Insurance Company, and had meant no slight.

"I don't quite see that," I observed.

"Don't see what?"

"How the world contrived to get so deeply into your debt — how all the points of the compass managed it."

"Thomas, I did n't ask to be born, did I?"

"Probably not."

"But I was born, was n't I?"

"To all appearances."

"Well, then!"

"But you cannot hold the world in general responsible for your birth. The responsibility narrows itself down to your parents."

"Then I am euchred. By one of those laws of nature which make this globe a sweet spot to live on, they were taken from me just when I needed them most — my mother in my infancy, and my father in my childhood."

"But your father left you something?"

"The old gentleman left me nothing, and I've been steadily increasing the legacy ever since."

"What did you do before the war?" inquired Clara sympathetically. His mention of his early losses had touched her.

"Oh, a number of things. I read law for a while. At one time I was interested in a large concern for the manufacture of patent metallic burial cases; but nobody seemed to die that year. Good health raged like an epidemic all over the South. Latterly I dabbled a little in stocks — and stocks dabbled in me."

"You were not successful, then?" I said.

"I was at first, but when the war fever broke out and the Southern heart was fired, everything that did n't go down went up."

"And you could n't meet your obligations?"

"That was n't the trouble — I could n't get away from them," replied the colonel, with a winsome smile. "I met them at every corner."

The man had a fashion of turning his very misfortunes into pleasantries. Surely prosperity would be wasted on a person so gifted with optimism. I felt it to be kind and proper,. however, to express the hope that he had reached the end of his adversity, and to assure him that I would do anything I could in the world to help him.

"Tom Wesley, I believe you would."

Before the close of that day Mrs. Wesley, who is a lady that does not allow any species of vegetation to accumulate under her feet, had secured a furnished room for our kinsman in a street branching off from Clinton Place, and at a moderate additional expense contracted to have him served with breakfasts on the premises. Previous to this I had dined down town, returning home in the evening to a rather heavy tea, which was really my wife's dinner — Sheridan and Ulysses (such were the heroic names under which the two little Wesleys were staggering) had their principal meal at midday.   It was, of course, not desirable that the colonel should share this meal with them and Mrs. Wesley in my absence.   So we decided to have a six-o'clock dinner; a temporary disarrangement of our domestic machinery, for my cousin Flagg would doubtless find some acceptable employment before long, and leave the household free to slip back into its regular grooves.

An outline of the physical aspects of the exotic kinsman who had so unexpectedly added himself to the figures at our happy fireside seems not out of place here. The portrait, being the result of many sittings, does not in some points convey the exact impression he made upon us in the earlier moments of our intimacy; but that is not important.

Though Washington Flagg had first opened his eyes on the banks of the Penobscot, he appeared to have been planned by nature to adorn the banks of the Rappahannock. There was nothing of the New-Englander about him. The sallowness of his complexion and the blackness of his straight hair, which he wore long, were those of the typical Southerner. He was of medium height and loosely built, with a kind of elastic grace in his disjointedness. When he smiled he was positively handsome; in repose his features were nearly plain, the lips too indecisive, and the eyes lacking in lustre. A sparse tuft of beard at his chin — he was otherwise smoothly shaven — lengthened the face. There was, when he willed it, something very ingratiat-

ing in his manner — even Clara admitted
that — a courteous and unconventional sort
of ease. In all these surface characteristics
he was a geographical anomaly. In the
cast of his mind he was more Southern than
the South, as a Northern convert is apt to
be. Even his speech, like the dyer's arm,
had taken tints from his environment. One
might say that his pronunciation had lit-
erally been colored by his long association
with the colored race. He invariably said
flo' for floor, and *djew* for dew; but I do
not anywhere attempt a phonetic reproduction of his dialect; in its finer qualities it
was too elusive to be snared in a network
of letters. In spite of his displacements,
for my cousin had lived all over the South
in his boyhood, he had contrived to pick up
a very decent education. As to his other
attributes, he shall be left to reveal them
himself.

III

Mrs. Wesley kindly assumed the charge
of establishing Washington Flagg in his
headquarters, as he termed the snug hall
bedroom in Macdougal Street. There were
numberless details to be looked to. His
wardrobe, among the rest, needed replenish-
ing down to the most unconsidered button,
for Flagg had dropped into our little world
with as few impedimenta as if he had been
a newly born infant. Though my condition,
like that desired by Agur, the son of Jakeh,
was one of neither poverty nor riches,
greenbacks in those days were greenbacks.
I mention the fact in order to say that my
satisfaction in coming to the rescue of my
kinsman would have been greatly lessened
if it had involved no self-denial whatever.

The day following his installation I was
partly annoyed, partly amused, to find that
Flagg had purchased a rather expensive

meerschaum pipe and a pound or two of Latakia tobacco.

" I cannot afford to smoke cigars," he explained. " I must economize until I get on my feet."

Perhaps it would have been wiser if I had personally attended to his expenditures, minor as well as major, but it did not seem practicable to leave him without a cent in his pocket. His pilgrimage down town that forenoon had apparently had no purpose beyond this purchase, though on the previous evening I had directed his notice to two or three commercial advertisements which impressed me as worth looking into. I hesitated to ask him if he had looked into them.   A collateral feeling of delicacy prevented me from breathing a word to Clara about the pipe.

Our reconstructed household, with its unreconstructed member, now moved forward on the lines laid down.   Punctually at a quarter to six P. M. my cousin appeared at the front door, hung his hat on the rack, and passed into the sitting-room, sometimes humming in the hall a bar or two of "The Bonny Blue Flag that bears a Single Star," to the infinite distaste of Mrs. Wesley, who was usually at that moment giving the finishing touches to the dinner table. After dinner, during which I was in a state of unrelaxed anxiety lest the colonel should get himself on too delicate ground, I took him into my small snuggery at the foot of the hall, where coffee was served to us, Mrs. Wesley being left to her own devices.

For several days everything went smoothly, beyond my hope. I found it so easy, when desirable, to switch the colonel on to one of my carefully contrived side tracks that I began to be proud of my skill and to enjoy the exercise of it. But one evening, just as we were in the middle of the dessert, he suddenly broke out with, "We were conquered by mere brute force, you know!"

"That is very true," I replied. "It is brute force that tells in war. Was n't it Napoleon who said that he had remarked that God was generally on the side which had the heaviest artillery?"

"The North had that, fast enough, and crushed a free people with it."

"A free people with four millions of slaves?" observed Mrs. Wesley quietly.

"Slavery was a patriarchal institution, my dear lady. But I reckon it is exploded now. The Emancipation Proclamation was a dastardly war measure."

"It did something more and better than free the blacks," said Mrs. Wesley; "it freed the whites. Dear me!" she added, glancing at Sheridan and Ulysses, who, in a brief reprieve from bed, were over in one corner of the room dissecting a small wooden camel, "I cannot be thankful enough that the children are too young to understand such sentiments."

The colonel, to my great relief, remained silent; but as soon as Clara had closed the dining-room door behind her, he said, "Tom Wesley, I reckon your wife does n't wholly like me."

"She likes you immensely," I cried, inwardly begging to be forgiven. "But she is a firm believer in the justice of the Northern cause."

"Maybe she lost a brother, or something."

"No; she never had a brother. If she had had one, he would have been killed in the first battle of the war. She sent me to the front to be killed, and I went willingly; but I was n't good enough; the enemy would n't have me at any price after a year's trial. Mrs. Wesley feels very strongly on this subject, and I wish you would try, like a good fellow, not to bring the question up at dinner - time. I am squarely opposed to your views myself, but I don't mind what you say as she does. So talk to me as much as you want to, but don't talk in Clara's presence. When persons disagree as you two do, argument is useless. Besides, the whole thing has been settled on the battle-field, and it is n't worth while to fight it all over again on a table-cloth."

"I suppose it is n't," he assented good-naturedly. "But you people up at the North here don't suspicion what we have been through. You caught only the edge of the hurricane.   The most of you, I take it, were n't in it at all."

" Our dearest were in it."

" Well, we got whipped, Wesley, I acknowledge it; but we deserved to win, if ever bravery deserved it."

" The South was brave, nobody contests that; but ' 't is not enough to be brave ' —

> ' The angry valor dashed
> On the awful shield of God,'

as one of our poets says."

" Blast one of your poets !   Our people were right, too."

" Come, now, Flagg, when you talk about your people, you ought to mean Northerners, for you were born in the North."

" That was just the kind of luck that has followed me all my life.   My body belongs to Bangor, Maine, and my soul to Charleston, South Carolina."

" You 've got a problem there that ought to bother you."

" It does," said the colonel, with a laugh.

" Meanwhile, my dear boy, don't distress Mrs. Wesley with it.   She is ready to be

very fond of you, if you will let her. It
would be altogether sad and shameful if a
family so contracted as ours could n't get
along without internal dissensions."

My cousin instantly professed the greatest regard for Mrs. Wesley, and declared
that both of us were good enough to be
Southrons. He promised that in future he
would take all the care he could not to run
against her prejudices, which merely grew
out of her confused conception of State
rights and the right of self-government.
Women never understood anything about
political economy and government, anyhow.

Having accomplished thus much with the
colonel, I turned my attention, on his departure, to smoothing Clara. I reminded
her that nearly everybody North and South
had kinsmen or friends in both armies. To
be sure, it was unfortunate that we, having
only one kinsman, should have had him on
the wrong side. That was better than having no kinsman at all. (Clara was inclined
to demur at this.) It had not been practicable for him to divide himself; if it had

been, he would probably have done it, and the two halves would doubtless have arrayed themselves against each other. They would, in a manner, have been bound to do so. However, the war was over, we were victorious, and could afford to be magnanimous.

"But he does n't seem to have discovered that the war is over," returned Clara. "He 'still waves.'"

"It is likely that certain obstinate persons on both sides of Mason and Dixon's line will be a long time making the discovery. Some will never make it — so much the worse for them and the country."

Mrs. Wesley meditated and said nothing, but I saw that so far as she and the colonel were concerned the war was not over.

IV

THIS slight breeze cleared the atmosphere
for the time being. My cousin Flagg took
pains to avoid all but the most indirect
allusions to the war, except when we were
alone, and in several small ways endeavored
— with not too dazzling success — to be
agreeable to Clara. The transparency of
the effort was perhaps the partial cause of
its failure. And then, too, the nature of his
little attentions was not always carefully
considered on his part. For example, Mrs.
Wesley could hardly be expected to lend
herself with any grace at all to the proposal
he made one sultry June evening to "knock
her up" a mint-julep, "the most refreshing
beverage on earth, madam, in hot weather,
I can assure you." Judge Ashburton Todhunter, of Fauquier County, had taught
him to prepare this pungent elixir from
a private receipt for which the judge had

once refused the sum of fifty dollars, offered
to him by Colonel Stanley Bluegrass, of
Chattanooga, and this was at a moment,
too, when the judge had been losing very
heavily at draw poker.

"All quiet along the Potomac," whispered the colonel, with a momentary pride
in the pacific relations he had established
between himself and Mrs. Wesley.

As the mint and one or two other necessary ingredients were lacking to our family
stores, the idea of julep was dismissed as a
vain dream, and its place supplied by iced
Congress water, a liquid which my cousin
characterized, in a hasty aside to me, as
being a drink fit only for imbecile infants
of a tender age.

Washington Flagg's frequent and familiar mention of governors, judges, colonels, and majors clearly indicated that he
had moved in aristocratic latitudes in the
South, and threw light on his disinclination
to consider any of the humbler employ-
ments which might have been open to him.
He had so far conceded to the exigency of

the case as to inquire if there were a possible chance for him in the Savonarola Fire Insurance Company. He had learned of my secretaryship. There was no vacancy in the office, and if there had been, I would have taken no steps to fill it with my cousin. He knew nothing of the business. Besides, however deeply I had his interests at heart, I should have hesitated to risk my own situation by becoming sponsor for so unmanageable an element as he appeared to be.

At odd times in my snuggery after dinner Flagg glanced over the "wants" columns of the evening journal, but never found anything he wanted. He found many amusing advertisements that served him as pegs on which to hang witty comment, but nothing to be taken seriously. I ventured to suggest that he should advertise. He received the idea with little warmth.

" No, my dear boy, I can't join the long procession of scullions, cooks, butlers, valets, and bottle - washers which seem to

make up so large a part of your population. I could n't keep step with them. It
is altogether impossible for me to conduct
myself in this matter like a menial-of-all-
work out of place. ' Wanted, a situation,
by a respectable young person of temper-
ate habits ; understands the care of horses ;
is willing to go into the country and milk
the cow with the crumpled horn.' No ;
many thanks."

" State your own requirements, Flagg.
I did n't propose that you should offer
yourself as coachman."

" It would amount to the same thing,
Wesley. I should at once be relegated
to his level. Some large opportunity is
dead sure to present itself to me if I wait.
I believe the office should seek the man."

" I have noticed that a man has to meet
his opportunities more than half way, or
he does n't get acquainted with them. Mohammed was obliged to go to the mountain,
after waiting for the mountain to come to
him."

" Mohammed's mistake was that he

did n't wait long enough. He was too impatient. But don't you fret. I have come to Yankeedom to make my fortune. The despot's heel is on your shore, and it means to remain there until he hears of something greatly to his advantage."

A few days following this conversation, Mr. Nelson, of Files and Nelson, wholesale grocers on Front Street, mentioned to me casually that he was looking for a shipping-clerk. Before the war the firm had done an extensive Southern trade, which they purposed to build up again now that the ports of the South were thrown open. The place in question involved a great deal of outdoor work — the loading and unloading of spicy cargoes, a life among the piers — all which seemed to me just suited to my cousin's woodland nature. I could not picture him nailed to a desk in a counting-room. The salary was not bewildering, but the sum was to be elastic, if ability were shown. Here was an excellent chance, a stepping-stone, at all events ; perhaps the large opportunity itself, artfully disguised as fifteen dollars a week. I spoke of Flagg to Mr. Nelson, and arranged a meeting between them for the next day.

I said nothing of the matter at the dinner table that evening; but an encouraging thing always makes a lantern of me, and Clara saw the light in my face. As soon as dinner was over I drew my cousin into the little side room, and laid the affair before him.

" And I have made an appointment for you to meet Mr. Nelson to-morrow at one o'clock," I said, in conclusion.

" My dear Wesley " — he had listened to me in silence, and now spoke without enthusiasm — " I don't know what you were thinking of to do anything of the sort. I will not keep the appointment with that person. The only possible intercourse I could have with him would be to order groceries at his shop. The idea of a man who has moved in the best society of the South, who has been engaged in great if unsuccessful enterprises, who has led the picked chivalry of his oppressed land

against the Northern hordes — the idea of
a gentleman of this kidney meekly simmer-
ing down into a factotum to a Yankee
dealer in canned goods ! No, sir ; I reckon
I can do better than that."

The lantern went out.

I resolved that moment to let my cousin
shape his own destiny — a task which in
no way appeared to trouble him. And,
indeed, now that I look back to it, why
should he have troubled himself ? He had
a comfortable if not luxurious apartment
in Macdougal Street ; a daily dinner that
asked only to be eaten ; a wardrobe that
was replenished when it needed replenish-
ing ; a weekly allowance that made up for
its modesty by its punctuality. If ever a
man was in a position patiently to await
the obsequious approach of large opportunities that man was Washington Flagg.
He was not insensible to the fact. He
passed his time serenely. He walked the
streets — Flagg was a great walker — sometimes wandering for hours in the Central
Park. His Southern life, passed partly

among plantations, had given him a relish for trees and rocks and waters. He was also a hungry reader of novels. When he had devoured our slender store of fiction, which was soon done, he took books from a small circulating library on Sixth Avenue. That he gave no thought whatever to the future was clear. He simply drifted down the gentle stream of the present. Sufficient to the day was the sunshine thereof.

In spite of his unforgivable inertia, and the egotism that enveloped him like an atmosphere, there was a charm to the man that put my impatience to sleep. I tried to think that this indifference and sunny idleness were perhaps the natural reaction of that larger life of emotion and activity from which he had just emerged. I reflected a great deal on that life, and, though I lamented the fact that he had drawn his sword on the wrong side, there was, down deep in my heart, an involuntary sympathetic throb for the valor that had not availed. I suppose the inexplicable ties of kinship had something to do with all this.

Washington Flagg had now been with us five weeks. He usually lingered awhile after dinner; sometimes spent the entire evening with the family, or, rather, with me, for Mrs. Wesley preferred the sitting-room to my den when I had company. Besides, there were Sheridan and Ulysses to be looked to. Toward the close of the sixth week I noticed that Flagg had fallen into a way of leaving immediately after dinner. He had also fallen into another way not so open to pleasant criticism.

By degrees — by degrees so subtle as almost to escape measurement — he had glided back to the forbidden and danger-ous ground of the war. At first it was an intangible reference to something that oc-curred on such and such a date, the date in question being that of some sanguinary battle; then a swift sarcasm, veiled and softly shod; then a sarcasm that dropped its veil for an instant, and showed its sharp features. At last his thought wore no dis-guise. Possibly the man could not help it; possibly there was something in the atmos-

phere of the house that impelled him to
say things which he would have been unlikely to say elsewhere. Whatever was the
explanation, my cousin Flagg began to
make himself disagreeable again at meal-
times.

He had never much regarded my disap-
proval, and now his early ill-defined fear
of Mrs. Wesley was evaporated. He no
longer hesitated to indulge in his war reminiscences, which necessarily brought his
personal exploits under a calcium-light.
These exploits usually emphasized his intimacy with some of the more dashing Southern leaders, such as Stonewall Jackson and
Jeb Stuart and Mosby. We found ourselves practically conscripted in the Confederate army. We were taken on long
midnight rides through the passes of the
Cumberland Mountains and hurled on some
Federal outpost; we were made — a mere
handful as we were — to assault and carry
most formidable earthworks; we crossed
dangerous fords, and bivouacked under
boughs hung with weird gonfalons of gray

moss, slit here and there by the edge of
a star. Many a time we crawled stealthily
through tangled vines and shrubs to the
skirt of a wood, and across a fallen log
sighted the Yankee picket whose bayonet
point glimmered now and then far off in
the moonlight. We spent a great many
hours around the camp - fire counting our
metaphorical scalps.

One evening the colonel was especially
exasperating with anecdotes of Stonewall
Jackson, and details of what he said to the
general and what the general said to him.

"Stonewall Jackson often used to say
to me, 'George' — he always called me
George, in just that off - hand way —
'George, when we get to New York, you
shall have quarters in the Astor House, and
pasture your mare Spitfire in the park.'"

"That was very thoughtful of Stonewall Jackson," remarked Mrs. Wesley,
with the faintest little whiteness gathering
at the lips. "I am sorry that your late
friend did not accompany you to the city,
and personally superintend your settlement

here.   He would have been able to sur-
round you with so many more comforts
than you have in Macdougal Street."

The colonel smiled upon Clara, and made
a deprecating gesture with his left hand.
Nothing seemed to pierce his ironclad composure.   A moment afterward he returned
to the theme, and recited some verses called
" Stonewall Jackson's Way."   He recited
them very well.   One stanza lingers in my
memory : —

> " We see him now — the old slouched hat
>   Cocked o'er his brow askew,
>   The shrewd, dry smile, the speech so pat,
>   So calm, so blunt, so true.
>   The Blue-light Elder knows 'em well.
>   Says he : ' That 's Banks ; he 's fond of shell.
>   Lord save his soul ! we 'll give him — '   Well,
>   That 's Stonewall Jackson's way."

" His ways must have been far from
agreeable," observed my wife, " if that is
a sample of them."

After the colonel had taken himself off,
Mrs. Wesley, sinking wearily upon the
sofa, said, " I think I am getting rather
tired of Stonewall Jackson."

" We both are my dear ; and some of our corps commanders used to find him rather tiresome now and then. He was really a great soldier, Clara ; perhaps the greatest on the other side."

" I suppose he was ; but Flagg comes next — according to his own report. Why, Tom, if your cousin had been in all the battles he says he has, the man would have been killed ten times over. He 'd have had at least an arm or a leg shot off."

That Washington Flagg had all his limbs on was actually becoming a grievance to Mrs. Wesley.

The situation filled me with anxiety. Between my cousin's deplorable attitude and my wife's justifiable irritation, I was extremely perplexed. If I had had a dozen cousins, the solution of the difficulty would have been simple. But to close our door on our only kinsman was an intolerable alternative.

If any word of mine has caused the impression that Clara was not gentle and sympathetic and altogether feminine, I have wronged her.   The reserve which strangers mistook for coldness was a shell that melted at the slightest kind touch, her masterful air the merest seeming.   But whatever latent antagonism lay in her nature the colonel had the faculty of bringing to the surface.   It must be conceded that the circumstances in which she was placed were trying, and Clara was without that strong, perhaps abnormal, sense of relationship which sustained me in the ordeal.   Later on, when matters grew more complicated, I could but admire her resignation — if it were not helpless despair.   Sometimes, indeed, she was unable to obliterate herself, and not only stood by her guns, but carried the war into the enemy's country.   I very frequently found myself between two fires, and was glad to drag what small fragments were left of me from the scene of action.   In brief, the little house in Clinton Place was rapidly transforming itself into a ghastly caricature of home.

Up to the present state of affairs the colonel had never once failed to appear at dinner-time. We had become so accustomed to his ring at the prescribed hour, and to hearing him outside in the hall softly humming "The Bonny Blue Flag," or, "I wish I was in Dixie's Land" (a wish which he did not wholly monopolize) — we had, I repeat, become so accustomed to these details that one night when he absented himself we experienced a kind of alarm. It was not until the clock struck ten that we gave over expecting him. Then, fearing that possibly he was ill, I put on my hat and stepped round to Macdougal Street. Mr. Flagg had gone out late in the afternoon, and had not returned. No, he had left no word in case any one called. What had happened? I smile to myself now, and I have smiled a great many times, at the remembrance of how worried I was that night as I walked slowly back to Clinton Place.

The next evening my cousin explained his absence. He had made the acquaintance of some distinguished literary gentlemen, who had invited him to dine with

them at a certain German café, which at an
earlier date had been rather famous as the
rendezvous of a group of young journalists,
wits, and unblossomed poets, known as
" The Bohemians." The war had caused
sad havoc with these light-hearted Knights
of the Long Table, and it was only upon a
scattered remnant of the goodly company
that the colonel had fallen. How it came
about, I do not know. I know that the acquaintance presently flowered into intimacy,
and that at frequent intervals after this we
had a vacant chair at table. My cousin did
not give himself the pains to advise us of
his engagements, so these absences were
not as pleasant as they would have been if
we had not expected him every minute.

Recently, too, our expectation of his
coming was tinged with a dread which
neither I nor Mrs. Wesley had named to
each other. A change was gradually taking
place in my cousin. Hitherto his amiabil-
ity, even when he was most unendurable,
had been a part of him. Obviously he was
losing that lightness of spirit which we once

disliked and now began to regret. He was
inclined to be excitable and sullen by turns,
and often of late I had been obliged to go
to the bottom of my diplomacy in prevent-
ing some painful scene. As I have said,
neither my wife nor I had spoken definitely
of this alteration; but the cause and nature
of it could not long be ignored between us.

" How patient you are with him, dear! "
said Mrs. Wesley, as I was turning out the
gas after one of our grim and grotesque
little dinners: the colonel had not dined
with us before for a week. " I don't see
how you can be so patient with the man."

" Blood is thicker than water, Clara."

" But it is n't thicker than whiskey and
water, is it ? "

She had said it. The colonel was drink-
ing. It was not a question of that light
elixir the precious receipt for which had
been confided to him by Judge Ashburton
Todhunter, of Fauquier County; it was a
question of a heavier and more immediate
poison. The fact that Flagg might in some
desperate state drop in on us at any mo-

ment stared us in the face. That was a
very serious contingency, and it was one I
could not guard against. I had no false
ideas touching my influence over Washington Flagg. I did not dream of attempting
to influence him; I was powerless. I could
do nothing but wait, and wonder what
would happen. There was nothing the man
might not be capable of in some insane
moment.

In the mean while I was afraid to go out
of an evening and leave Clara alone. It
was impossible for us to ask a friend to
dinner, though, indeed, we had not done
that since my cousin dropped down on us.
It was no relief that his visits grew rarer
and rarer; the apprehension remained. It
was no relief when they ceased altogether,
for it came to that at last.

A month had elapsed since he had called
at the house. I had caught sight of him
once on Broadway as I was riding up town
in an omnibus. He was standing at the top
of the steep flight of steps that led to Herr
Pfaff's saloon in the basement. It was

probably Flagg's dinner hour. Mrs. Morgan, the landlady in Macdougal Street, a melancholy little soul, was now the only link between me and my kinsman. I had a weekly interview with her. I learned that Mr. Flagg slept late, was seldom in during the day, and usually returned after midnight. A person with this eccentric scheme of life was not likely to be at home at such hours as I might find it convenient to call. Nevertheless, from time to time I knocked at the unresponsive door of his room. The two notes I had written to him he left unanswered.

All this was very grievous. He had been a trouble to me when I had him, and he was a trouble to me now I had lost him. My trouble had merely changed its color. On what downward way were his footsteps? What was to be the end of it? Sometimes I lay awake at night thinking of him. Of course, if he went to the dogs, he had nobody to blame but himself. I was not responsible for his wrong-going; nevertheless, I could not throw off my anxiety in the matter. That Flagg was leading a wild life in these days was presumable. Indeed, certain rumors to that effect were indirectly blown to me from the caves of Gambrinus. Not that I believe the bohemians demoralized him. He probably demoralized the bohemians. I began to reflect whether fate had not behaved rather handsomely, after all, in not giving me a great many relatives.

If I remember rightly, it was two months since I had laid eyes on my cousin, when, on returning home one evening, I noticed that the front door stood wide open, and had apparently been left to take care of itself. As I mounted the steps, a little annoyed at Mary's carelessness, I heard voices in the hall. Washington Flagg was standing at the foot of the staircase, with his hand on the newel-post, and Mrs. Wesley was half-way up the stairs, as if in the act of descending. I learned later that she had occupied this position for about three quarters of an hour. She was extremely pale and much agitated. Flagg's flushed face and tilted hat told his part of the story.

He was not in one of his saturnine moods. He was amiably and, if I may say it, gracefully drunk, and evidently had all his wits about him.

"I've been telling Mrs. Wesley," he began at once, as if I had been present all the while, and he was politely lifting me into the conversation — "I've been telling Mrs. Wesley that I'm a Lost Cause."

"A lost soul," was Mrs. Wesley's amendment from the staircase. "Oh, Tom, I am so glad you have come! I thought you never would! I let him in an hour or two ago, and he has kept me here ever since."

"You were so entertaining," said my cousin, with a courteous sweep of his disengaged hand, and speaking with that correctness of enunciation which sometimes survives everything.

"Flagg," I said, stepping to his side, "you will oblige me by returning to your lodgings."

"You think I'm not all right?"

"I am sure of it."

"And you don't want me here, dear old boy?"

"No, I don't want you here. The time has come for me to be frank with you, Flagg, and I see that your mind is clear enough to enable you to understand what I say."

"I reckon I can follow you, Thomas."

"My stock of romantic nonsense about kinship and family duties, and all that, has given out, and will not be renewed."

"Won't do business any more at the old stand?"

"Exactly so. I have done everything I could to help you, and you have done nothing whatever for yourself. You have not even done yourself the scant justice of treating Clara and me decently. In future you will be obliged to look after your own affairs, financial as well as social. Your best plan now is to go to work. I shall no longer concern myself with your comings and goings, except so far as to prevent you from coming here and disturbing Clara. Have you put that down?"

"Wesley, my boy, I'll pay you for this."

"If you do, it will be the first thing you have paid for since you came North."

My statement, however accurate, was not wholly delicate, and I subsequently regretted it, but when a patient man loses his patience he goes to extremes. Washington Flagg straightened himself for an instant, and then smiled upon me in an amused, patronizing way quite untranslatable.

" Thomas, that was neat, very neat — for you. When I see Judge Ashburton Todhunter I 'll tell him about it. It 's the sort of mild joke he likes."

" I should be proud to have Judge Ashburton Todhunter's approval of any remark of mine, but in the mean while it would be a greater pleasure to me to have you return at once to Macdougal Street, where, no doubt, Mrs. Morgan is delaying dinner for you."

" Say no more, Wesley. I 'll never set foot in your house again, as sure as my name is Flagg — and long may I wave o'er the land of the free and the home of the brave."

" He is a kind of Flagg that I don't wish to have wave over *my* home," said Mrs.

Wesley, descending the stairs as my cousin with painful care closed the door softly behind him.

So the end was come. It had come with less unpleasantness than I should have predicted. The ties of kindred, too tightly stretched, had snapped; but they had snapped very gently, so to speak.

V

WASHINGTON FLAGG was as good as his word, which is perhaps not a strong indorsement. He never again set foot in my house. A week afterward I found that he had quitted Macdougal Street.

"He has gone South," said Mrs. Morgan.

"Did he leave no message for me?"

"He did n't leave a message for nobody."

"Did he happen to say to what part of the South he was bound?"

"He said he was going back to Dixie's land, and did n't say no more."

That was all. His departure had been as abrupt and unlooked-for as his arrival. I wondered if he would turn up again at the end of another twenty years, and I wondered how he had paid his traveling expenses to the land of the magnolia and the persimmon. That mystery was solved a few days subsequently when a draft (for so reasonable a sum as not to be worth mentioning to Clara) was presented to me for payment at my office.

Washington Flagg was gone, but his shadow was to linger for a while longer on our household. It was difficult to realize that the weight which had oppressed us had been removed. We were scarcely conscious of how heavy it had been until it was lifted. I was now and then forced to make an effort not to expect the colonel to dinner.

A month or two after his disappearance an incident occurred which brought him back very vividly and in a somewhat sinister shape to our imaginations. Quite late one night there was a sharp ring at the door. Mary having gone to bed, I answered the bell. On the doorstep stood a tall, pale girl, rather shabbily dressed, but with a kind of beauty about her; it seemed to flash from her eyelashes, which I noticed were very heavy. The hall light fell full upon this slight figure, standing there wrapped in an insufficient shawl, against a dense background of whirling snow-flakes. She asked if I could give her Colonel Flagg's address. On receiving my reply, the girl swiftly descended the steps, and vanished into the darkness. There was a tantalizing point of romance and mystery to all this. As I slowly closed the front door I felt that perhaps I was closing it on a tragedy — one of those piteous, unwritten tragedies of the great city. I have wondered a thousand times who that girl was and what became of her.

Before the end of the year another incident — this time with a touch of comedy — lighted up the past of my kinsman. Among the traveling agents for the Savonarola Fire Insurance Company was a young man by the name of Brett, Charles Brett, a new employé. His family had been ruined by the war, and he had wandered North, as the son of many a Southern gentleman had been obliged to do, to earn his living. We became friends, and frequently lunched together when his business brought him to the city. Brett had been in the Confederate army, and it occurred to me one day to ask him if he had ever known my cousin the colonel. Brett was acquainted with a George W. Flagg; had known him somewhat intimately, in fact; but it was probably not the same man. We compared notes, and my Flagg was his Flagg.

"But he wasn't a colonel," said Brett. "Why, Flagg wasn't in the war at all. I don't fancy he heard a gun fired, unless it went off by accident in some training-camp for recruits. He got himself exempt from service in the field by working in the government saltworks. A heap of the boys escaped conscription that way."

In the saltworks! That connected my cousin with the navy rather than with the army!

I would have liked not to believe Brett's statement, but it was so circumstantial and precise as not to be doubted. Brett was far from suspecting how deeply his information had cut me. In spite of my loyalty, the discovery that my kinsman had not been a full-blown rebel was vastly humiliating.

How that once curiously regarded flower of chivalry had withered! What about those reckless moonlight raids? What had become of Prince Rupert, at the head of his plumed cavaliers, sweeping through the valley of the Shenandoah, and dealing merited destruction to the boys in blue? In view of Brett's startling revelation, my kinsman's personal anecdotes of Stonewall Jackson took on an amusing quality which they had not possessed for us in the original telling.

I was disappointed that Clara's astonishment was much more moderate than mine.

"He was *too* brave, Tom, dear. He always seemed to be overdoing it just a grain, don't you think!"

I didn't think so at the time; I was afraid he was telling the truth. And now, by one of those contradictions inseparable from weak humanity, I regretted that he was not. A hero had tumbled from the family pedestal — a misguided hero, to be sure, but still a hero. My vanity, which in this case was of a complex kind, had received a shock.

I did not recover from it for nearly three months, when I received a second shock of a more serious nature. It came in the shape of a letter, dated at Pensacola, Florida, and written by one Sylvester K. Matthews, advising me that George Flagg had died of the yellow fever in that city on the previous month. I gathered from the letter that the writer had been with my cousin through his illness, and was probably an intimate friend; at all events, the details of the funeral had fallen to the charge of Mr. Matthews, who inclosed the receipted bills with the remark that he had paid them, but supposed that I would prefer to do so, leaving it, in a way,.at my option.

The news of my cousin's death grieved me more than I should have imagined beforehand. He had not appreciated my kindness; he had not added to my happiness while I was endeavoring to secure his; he had been flagrantly ungrateful, and in one or two minor matters had deceived me. Yet, after all said and done, he was my cousin, my only cousin — and he was dead.

Let us criticise the living, but spare the
dead.

I put the memoranda back into the en-
velope; they consisted of a bill for medical attendance, a board bill, the nurse's
account, and an undertaker's bill, with its
pathetic and, to me, happily, unfamiliar
items. For the rest of the day I was unable to fix my attention on my work, or to
compose myself sufficiently to write to Mr.
Matthews. I quitted the office that evening an hour earlier than was my habit.

Whether Clara was deeply affected by
what had happened, or whether she dis-
approved of my taking upon myself expenses which, under the peculiar circumstances, might properly be borne by Flagg's
intimate friend and comrade, was something
I could not determine. She made no com-
ments. If she considered that I had already done all that my duty demanded of
me to do for my cousin, she was wise
enough not to say so; for she must have
seen that I took a different and unalterable
view of it. Clara has her own way fifty-

nine minutes out of the hour, but the
sixtieth minute is mine.

She was plainly not disposed to talk on
the subject; but I wanted to talk with
some one on the subject; so, when dinner
was through, I put the Matthews papers
into my pocket and went up to my friend
Bleeker's, in Seventeenth Street. Though
a little cynical at times, he was a man
whose judgment I thought well of.

After reading the letter and glancing
over the memoranda, Bleeker turned to
me and said, "You want to know how it
strikes me — is that it?"

"Well — yes."

"The man is dead?"

"Yes."

"And buried?"

"Assuredly."

"And the bills are paid?"

"You see yourself they are receipted."

"Well, then," said Bleeker, "consider-
ing all things, I should let well enough
alone."

"You mean you would do nothing in
the matter?"

"I should 'let the dead past bury its dead,' as Longfellow says." Bleeker was always quoting Longfellow.

"But it is n't the dead past, it 's the living present that has attended to the business; and he has sent in his account with all the items. I can't have this Matthews going about the country telling everybody that I allowed him to pay my cousin's funeral expenses."

"Then pay them. You have come to me for advice after making up your mind to follow your own course. That 's just the way people do when they really want to be advised. I 've done it myself, Wesley — I 've done it myself."

The result was, I sent Mr. Matthews a check, after which I impulsively threw those dreadful bills into the office grate. I had no right to do it, for the vouchers really belonged to Mr. Matthews, and might be wanted some day; but they had haunted me like so many ghosts until I destroyed them. I fell asleep that night trying to recollect whether the items in-

cluded a headstone for my cousin's grave.
I could n't for the life of me remember, and
it troubled me not a little. There were
enough nameless graves in the South, without his being added to the number.

One day, a fortnight later, as Clara and
I were finishing dinner, young Brett called
at the house. I had supposed him to be in
Omaha. He had, in effect, just come from
there and elsewhere on one of his long business tours, and had arrived in the city too
late in the afternoon to report himself at
the office. He now dropped in merely for
a moment, but we persuaded him to remain
and share the dessert with us. I purposed
to keep him until Clara left us to our cigars. I wished to tell him of my cousin's
death, which I did not care to do while she
was at the table. We were talking of this
and that, when Brett looked up, and said,
rather abruptly : —

" By the way, I saw Flagg on the street
the other day in Mobile. He was looking
well."

The bit of melon I had in my mouth

refused to be swallowed. I fancy that my face was a study. A dead silence followed; and then my wife reached across the table, and pressing my hand, said, very gently, —

"Wesley, you were not brilliant, but you were good."

All this was longer ago than I care to remember. I heard no more from Mr. Matthews. Last week, oddly enough, while glancing over a file of recent Southern newspapers, I came across the announcement of the death of George W. Flagg. It was yellow fever this time also. If later on I receive any bills in connection with that event, I shall let my friend Bleeker audit them.

A CHRISTMAS FANTASY, WITH A MORAL

HER name was Mildred Wentworth, and she lived on the slope of Beacon Hill, in one of those old-fashioned swell-front houses which have the inestimable privilege of looking upon Boston Common. It was Christmas afternoon, and she had gone up to the blue room, on the fourth floor, in order to make a careful inspection in solitude of the various gifts that had been left in her slender stocking and at her bedside the previous night.

Mildred was in some respects a very old child for her age, which she described as being "half past seven," and had a habit of spending hours alone in the large front chamber occupied by herself and the governess. This day the governess had gone to keep Christmas with her own family in South Boston, and it so chanced that Mildred had been left to dispose of her time as she pleased during the entire afternoon. She was well content to have the opportunity, for fortune had treated her magnificently, and it was deep satisfaction, after the excitement of the morning, to sit in the middle of that spacious room, with its three windows overlooking the pearl-crusted trees in the Common, and examine her treasures without any chance of interruption.

The looms of Cashmere and the workshops of Germany, the patient Chinamen and the irresponsible polar bear, had alike contributed to those treasures. Among other articles was a small square box, covered with mottled paper and having an outlandish, mysterious aspect, as if it belonged to a magician. When you loosened the catch of this box, possibly supposing it to contain bonbons of a superior quality, there sprang forth a terrible little monster, with a drifting white beard like a snow-storm, round emerald-green eyes, and a pessimistic expression of countenance generally, as though he had been reading Tolstoi or Schopenhauer.

This abrupt personage, whose family name was Heliogabalus, was known for simplicity's sake as Jumping Jack; and though the explanation of the matter is beset with difficulties, it is not to be concealed that he held a higher place in the esteem of Miss Wentworth than any of her other possessions, not excluding a tall wax doll *fin de siècle*, with a pallid complexion and a profusion of blonde hair. Titania was not more in love with Nick Bottom the weaver than Mildred with Jumping Jack. It was surely not his personal beauty that won her, for he had none; it was not his intellect, for intellect does not take up its abode in a forehead of such singular construction as that of Jumping Jack. But whatever the secret charm was, it worked. On a more realistic stage than this we see analogous cases every day. Perhaps Oberon still exercises his fairy craft in our material world, and scatters at will upon the eyelids of mortals the magic distillation of that "little Western flower" which

> "Will make or man or woman madly dote
> Upon the next live creature that it sees."

For an hour or so Mildred amused herself sufficiently by shutting Heliogabalus up in the chest and letting him spring out again; then she grew weary of the diversion, and finally began to lose patience with her elastic companion because he was unable to crowd himself into the box and undo the latch with his own fingers. This was extremely unreasonable; but so was Mildred made.

"How tedious you are!" she cried, at last. "You dull little old man, I don't see how I ever came to like you. I don't like you any more, with your glass eyes, and your silly pink mouth always open and never saying the least thing. What do you mean, sir, by standing and staring at me in that tiresome way? You look enough like Dobbs the butcher to be his brother, or to be Dobbs himself. I wonder you don't up

and say, 'Steaks or chops, mum?' Dear
me! I wish you really had some life in
you, and could move about, and talk with
me, and make yourself agreeable. Do be
alive!"

Mildred gave a little laugh at her own
absurdity, and then, being an imaginative
creature, came presently to regard the idea
as not altogether absurd, and, finally, as not
absurd at all. If a bough that has been
frozen to death all winter can put forth
blossoms in the spring, why might not an
inanimate object, which already possessed
many of the surface attributes of humanity,
and possibly some of the internal mechanism, add to itself the crowning gift of
speech? In view of the daily phenomena
of existence, would that be so very astonish-
ing? Of course the problem took a simpler
shape than this in Mildred's unsophisticated
thought.

She folded her hands in her lap, and,
rocking to and fro, reflected how pleasant
it would be if Jumping Jack, or her doll,
could come to life, like the marble lady in

the play, and do some of the talking. What
wonderful stories Jumping Jack would have
to tell, for example. He must have had no
end of remarkable adventures before he
lost his mind. Probably the very latest
intelligence from Lilliput was in his possession, and perhaps he was even now vainly
trying to deliver himself of it. His fixed,
open mouth hinted as much. The Land of
the Pygmies, in the heart of Darkest Africa
— just then widely discussed in the newspapers — was of course familiar ground to
him. How interesting it would be to learn,
at first hand, of the manners and customs
of those little folk. Doubtless he had been
a great traveler in foreign parts; the label,
in German text, on the bottom of his trunk
showed that he had recently come from
Munich. Munich! What magic there was
in the very word! As Mildred rocked to
and fro, her active little brain weaving the
most grotesque fancies, a drowsiness stole
over her. She was crooning to herself
fainter and fainter, and every instant drifting nearer to the shadowy reefs on the

western coast of Nowhere, when she heard a soft, inexplicable rustling sound close at her side. Mildred lifted her head quickly, just in time to behold Heliogabalus describe a graceful curve in the air and land lightly in the midst of her best Dresden china tea-set.

"Ho, ho!" he cried, in a voice preternaturally gruff for an individual not above five inches in height. "Ho, ho!" And he immediately began to throw Mildred's cups and saucers and plates all about the apartment.

"Oh, you horrid, wicked little man!" cried Mildred, starting to her feet. "Stop it!"

"Oh, you cross little girl!" returned the dwarf, with his family leer. "You surprise me!" And another plate crashed against the blue-flowered wall-paper.

"Stop it!" she repeated; and then to herself, "It's a mercy I waked up just when I did!"

"Patience, my child; I'm coming there shortly, to smooth your hair and kiss you."

"Do!" screamed Mildred, stooping to pick up a large Japanese crystal which lay absorbing the wintry sunlight at her feet.

When Heliogabalus saw that, he retired to the further side of his tenement, peeping cautiously over the top and around the corner, and disappearing altogether whenever Mildred threatened to throw the crystal at him. Now Miss Wentworth was naturally a courageous girl, and when she perceived that the pygmy was afraid of her she resolved to make an example of him. He was such a small affair that it really did not seem worth while to treat him with much ceremony. He had startled her at first, his manners had been so very violent; but now that her pulse had gone down she regarded him with calm curiosity, and wondered what he would do next.

"Listen," he said presently, in a queer, deferential way, as he partly emerged from his hiding-place; "I came to request the hand of mademoiselle yonder," and, nodding his head in the direction of Blondella, the doll, he retreated bashfully.

"Her?" cried Mildred, aghast.

"*You* are very nice, but I can't marry out of my own set, you know," observed Heliogabalus, invisible behind his breastwork. This shyness was mere dissimulation, as his subsequent behavior proved.

"Who would have thought it!" murmured Mildred to herself; and as she glanced suspiciously at Blondella, sitting bolt upright between the windows, with her back against the mopboard, Mildred fancied that she could almost detect a faint roseate hue stealing into the waxen cheek. "Who would have thought it!" And then, addressing Jumping Jack, she cried, "Come here directly; you audacious person!" and she stamped her foot in a manner that would have discouraged most suitors.

But Heliogabalus, who had now seated himself on the lid of his trunk and showed no trace of his late diffidence, smiled superciliously as he twisted off a bit of wire that protruded from the heel of one of his boots.

This effrontery increased Miss Wentworth's indignation, and likewise rather embarrassed her.   Perhaps he was not afraid of her after all.   In which case he was worth nothing as an example.

" I will brush you off, and tread on you," she observed tentatively, as if she were addressing an insect.

" Oh, indeed," he rejoined derisively, crossing his legs.

" I will ! " cried Mildred, making an impulsive dash at him.

Though taken at a disadvantage the manikin eluded her with surprising ease.   His agility was such as to render it impossible to determine whether he was an old young man or a very young old man.   Mildred eyed him doubtfully for a moment, and then gave chase.   Away went the quaint little figure, now darting under the brass bedstead, now dodging around the legs of the table, and now slipping between the feet of his pursuer at the instant she was on the point of laying hand on him.   Owing doubtless to some peculiarity of his articulation, each movement of his limbs was accompanied by a rustling wiry sound like the faint reverberation of a banjo-string somewhere in the distance.

Heliogabalus may have been a person with no great conversational gift, but his gymnastic acquirements were of the first order. Mildred not only could not catch him, but she could not restrain the manikin from meanwhile doing all kinds of desultory mischief; for in the midst of his course he would pause to overturn her tin kitchen, or shy a plate across the room, or give a vicious twitch to the lovely golden hair of Blondella, in spite of — perhaps in consequence of — his recent tender advances. It was plain that in eluding Mildred he was prompted by caprice rather than by fear.

"If things go on in this way," she reflected, "I sha'n't have anything left. If I could only get the dreadful little creature into a corner! There goes my tureen! What *shall* I do?"

To quit the room, even for a moment, in order to call for assistance at the head of the staircase, where, moreover, her voice was not likely to reach any one, was to leave everything at the mercy of that small demon. Mildred was out of breath with running, and ready to burst into tears with exasperation, when a different mode of procedure suggested itself to her. She would make believe that she was no longer angry, and perhaps she could accomplish by cunning what she had failed to compass by violence. She would consent — at least seem to consent — to let him marry Blondella, though he had lately given no signs of a very fervid attachment. Beyond this Mildred had no definite scheme, when the story of the Fisherman and the Evil Afrite flashed upon her memory from the pages of "The Arabian Nights." Her dilemma was exactly that of the unlucky fisherman, and her line of action should be the same, with such modification as the exigencies might demand. As in his case, too, there was no time to be lost. An expression of ineffable benevolence and serenity instantly overspread the features of Miss Wentworth. She leaned against the wardrobe, and regarded Jumping Jack with a look of gentle reproach.

"I thought you were going to be interesting," she remarked softly.

"Ain't I interesting?" asked the goblin, with a touch of pardonable sensitiveness.

"No," said Mildred candidly; "you are not. Perhaps you try to be. That's something, to be sure, though it's not everything. Oh, *I* don't want to touch you," she went on, with an indifferent toss of her curls. "How old are you?"

"Ever so old and ever so young."

"Truly? How very odd to be both at once! Can you read?"

"Never tried."

"I'm afraid your parents didn't bring you up very well," reflected Mildred.

"I speak all languages. The little folk of every age and every country understand me."

"You're a great traveler, then."

"I should say so!"

"You don't seem to carry much baggage

about with you. I suppose you belong
somewhere, and keep your clothes there. I
really should like to know where you came
from, if it's all the same to you."

"Out of that box, my dove," replied
Jumping Jack, having become affable in
his turn.

"Never!" exclaimed Mildred, with a delightful air of incredulity.

"I hope I may die," declared Heliogabalus, laying one hand on the left breast
of his mainspring.

"I don't believe it," said Mildred, con-
fidently.

"Ho, ho!"

"You are too tall, and too wide, and too
—fluffy. I don't mean to hurt your feelings, but you *are* fluffy. And I just want
you to stop that ho-hoing. No; I don't believe it."

"You don't, don't you? Behold!" And
placing both hands on the floor, Heliogabalus described a circle in the air, and
neatly landed himself in the box.

He was no sooner in than Mildred clapped

down the lid, and seated herself upon it victoriously. In the suddenness of her movement she had necessarily neglected to fasten the catch; but that was a detail that could be attended to later. Meanwhile she was mistress of the situation and could dictate terms. One thing was resolved: Jumping Jack was never to jump again. To-morrow he should be thrown into the Charles at the foot of Mount Vernon Street, in order that the tide might carry him out to sea. What would she not have given if she could have sealed him up with that talismanic Seal of Solomon which held the cruel marid so securely in his brazen casket? Of course it was not in Mildred's blood to resist the temptation to tease her captive a little.

"Now, Mr. Jack, I guess I've got you where you belong. If you are not an old man this very minute, you will be when you get out. You wanted to carry off my Blondella, did you? The idea! I hope you're quite comfortable."

"Let me out!" growled Heliogabalus in his deepest bass.

"I couldn't think of it, dear. You are one of those little boys that shouldn't be *either* seen or heard; and I don't want you to speak again, for I'm sitting on your head, and your voice goes right through me. So you will please remember not to speak unless you are spoken to." And Mildred broke into the merriest laugh imaginable, recollecting how many times she herself had been extinguished by the same instructions.

But Mildred's triumph was premature, for the little man in the box was as strong as a giant in a dime museum; and now that he had fully recovered his breath, he began pushing in a most systematic manner with his head and shoulders, and Mildred, to her great consternation, found herself being slowly lifted up on the lid of the chest, do what she might. In a minute or two more she must inevitably fall off, and Jumping Jack would have her! And what mercy could she expect at his hands, after her treatment of him! She was lost! Mildred stretched out her arms in despair, gave a shriek, and opened her eyes, which had been all the while as tightly shut as a couple of morning-glories at sundown.

She was sitting on a rug in the middle of the room. Though the window-panes were still flushed with the memory of the winter sunset, the iridescent lights had faded out in the Japanese crystal at her feet. She was not anywhere near the little imp. There he was over by the fireplace, staring at nothing in his usual senseless fashion. Not a piece of crockery had been broken, not a chair upset, and Blondella, the too-fascinating Blondella, had not had a single tress disarranged.

Mildred drew a long breath of relief. What had happened? Had she been dreaming? She was unable to answer the question; but as she abstractedly shook out the creases in the folds of her skirt, she remarked to herself that she did not care, on the whole, to have any of her things come to life, certainly not Jumping Jack. Just then the splintering of an icicle on the window-ledge outside sent a faint whiteness into her cheek, and caused her to throw a

quick, apprehensive glance toward the fireplace. After an instant's hesitation, Mildred, unconsciously dragging Blondella by
the hair, stole softly from the room, where
the spectres of the twilight were beginning
to gather rather menacingly, and went
downstairs to join the family and relate her
strange adventure.

The analysis of Miss Wentworth's dream
— if it were a dream, for later on she declared it was not, and hurriedly gave Heliogabalus to an unpleasant small boy who
lived next door — the analysis of her dream,
I repeat, shows strong traces of a moral.
Indeed the residuum is purely of that strin-
gent quality. Heliogabalus must be accepted as the symbol of an ill-considered
desire realized. The earnestness with which
Miss Wentworth invoked the phantasm
and the misery that came of it are a common experience. Painfully to attain possession of what we do not want, and then
painfully to waste our days in attempting
to rid ourselves of it, seems to be a part of

our discipline here below.   I know a great many excellent persons who are spending the latter moiety of life in the endeavor to get their particular Jumping Jack snugly back into its box again.

HER DYING WORDS

It was the good ship Agamenticus, five days out from New York, and bound for Liverpool. There was never a ship in a more pitiful plight.

On the Tuesday morning when she left Sandy Hook behind her, the sea had been nearly as smooth as an inland pond, and the sky one unbroken blue. What wind there was came in fitful puffs, and the captain began to be afraid that it would leave them altogether. Toward sunset, however, the breeze freshened smartly, and the vessel made a phenomenal run. On the following noon there was a falling barometer, the weather thickened, the sun went down in a purple blur, and by midnight the wind was blowing a gale. The next day the Agamenticus found herself rolling and plunging in the midst of one of those summer tempests which frequently can give points to their wintry accomplices. Captain Saltus, who had sailed the ocean for forty years, man and boy, had never experienced anything like that Thursday night, unless it was that Friday night, when nothing but a series of miracles saved the ship from foundering.

On Saturday morning the storm was over. The sun was breaking gorgeously through a narrow bank of fog that stretched from east to west, and the sea was calming itself, sullenly and reluctantly, with occasional moans and spasms. The storm was over, but it had given the Agamenticus her death-blow. The dripping decks were cluttered with rope-ends, split blocks, broken stanchions, and pine splinters — the débris of the foremast, of which only some ten or twenty feet remained. Such canvas as had not been securely furled hung in shreds from the main and mizzen yards, and at every lurch of the ship the flying cordage aloft lashed the masts. Two life-boats, with the bottoms stove in, swung loosely

from the davits on the port side ; the starboard boats were gone. The same sea that
had wrenched them from their fastenings
had also swept away John Sharon, the first
mate. But the climax of all these disas-
ters was a dreadful leak, the exact location
of which was hidden by the cargo.

Such was the plight of the good ship
Agamenticus at sunrise, on that fifth day
out from New York.

The Agamenticus was a merchantman of
about twelve hundred tons, and had excellent cabin accommodations, though she had
been designed especially for freight. On
this voyage, however, there happened to be
five passengers — Mr. and Mrs. Livingston
Tredick, Ellen Louise, their daughter, Dr.
Newton Downs, and Miss Tredick's maid.
The vessel belonged to a line running between Boston and New Orleans, and on
the present occasion was making a chance
trip to Liverpool.

Mr. Tredick was a wealthy retired mer-
chant who was intending to pass the summer
at the German baths with his wife and

daughter, and had followed the advice of his family physician in selecting a sailing vessel instead of a steamer, in order that Mrs. Tredick, somewhat of an invalid, might get the benefit of a protracted sea voyage. Louise, the daughter, was a very beautiful girl of nineteen or twenty ; and Dr. Downs was a young physician of great promise and few patients, who had willingly consented to be Mr. Tredick's guest as far as Liverpool. The air in which Miss Louise Tredick moved had been for two years or more the only air that this young scientist could breathe without difficulty.

The relations existing between these two persons were of a rather unusual nature, and require a word or so of explanation.

At the time of his father's death, which occurred in 1879, Newton Downs was in his senior year at Bowdoin. The father had been a lawyer with an extensive practice and extravagant tastes, and his large annual income, easily acquired, had always been as easily disposed of. He was still in his prime, and was meditating future econo-

mies for the sake of his boy, when death
placed an injunction on those plans. Young
Downs was left with little more than sufficient means to enable him to finish his
college course and pursue his medical studies for a year or two abroad. He then
established himself professionally in New
York; that is to say, he took a modest
suite of rooms on a ground floor in West
Eighteenth Street, and ornamented the
right-hand side of the doorway with an en-
graved brass plate

> Newton Downs, M. D.
> *Aurist.*

The small, semi-detached boy whose duty
it was to keep that brass tablet bright absorbed the whole of the Doctor's fees for
the first six months.

It was in the course of this tentative
first half year that Dr. Downs made the acquaintance of the Tredick family, and had
definitely surrendered himself to the charm
of Miss Tredick, before he discovered the

fact — to him the fatal fact — that she was
not only the daughter of a very wealthy father, but was very wealthy in her own right.
In the eyes of most men these offenses would
not have seemed without mitigating circumstances ; but to Dr. Downs, with his peculiar
point of view, they were an insurmounta-
ble barrier. A young and impoverished
gentleman, who had made a specialty of
the human ear and could not get any hearing out of the public, was scarcely a brilliant *parti* for Miss Ellen Louise Tredick.
His pride and his poverty, combined, closed
that gate on Dr. Downs.   If he could have
been poor and not proud, perhaps it would
have greatly simplified the situation.

 " Since fate has set me penniless on
the threshold of life," reflected the Doctor,
one evening shortly after his financial discovery, " why did not fate make a pauper
of Miss Tredick ?   Then I could have
asked her to be my wife, and faced the
world dauntlessly, like thousands of others
who have found love a sufficient capital
to start housekeeping on.   Miss Tredick's

grandfather behaved like an idiot, to go and leave her such a preposterous fortune; and her own father is not behaving himself much better. I wish the pair of them could lose their money. If Tredick only were a Wall Street magnate, there would be some chance of their going to pieces some fine day — then I might pick up one of the pieces!"

Unless he should become abruptly rich, or Mr. Tredick and his daughter abruptly poor, there really seemed no way out of it for the young doctor. As the months went by, neither of those things appeared likely to happen. So Newton Downs kept his love to himself, and looked with despairing eyes upon Miss Tredick as a glittering impossibility. It was the desire of the moth for the star, the longing of the dime to be a dollar.

Dr. Downs's unhappiness did not terminate here. There is no man at once so unselfish and selfish as a man in love. In this instance the moth, without the dimmest perception of its own ungenerosity, wanted

the star to be a little unhappy also.　There
was no sacrifice, excepting that of his pride,
which Dr. Downs would not have made for
Miss Tredick; yet he found it very hard
to have a hopeless passion all to himself,
and that, clearly, was what he was having.
He had no illusions concerning Miss
Tredick's attitude toward him.　It was
one of intimate indifference.　A girl does
not treat a possible lover with unvarying
simplicity and directness.　In all its phases
love is complex ; friendship is not.　With
other men Miss Tredick coquetted, or almost coquetted; but with him she never
dropped that air of mere *camaraderie* which
said as distinctly as such a disagreeable
thing ought ever to be said, " Of course,
between us *that* is out of the question. You
cannot offer me the kind of home you would
take me from, and I know you slightly, Dr.
Downs, if you would be willing to accept
rich surroundings at any woman's hand.　I
like you very much — in a way ; and papa
likes you very well, too.　He sees that you
are not at all sentimental."　Times without

number had Downs translated Miss Tredick's manner into these or similar phrases.
He came at last to find a morbid satisfaction in such literary exercises.

Now, Newton Downs had been under-
going this experience for upward of two
years, when Mr. Tredick, who appeared
indeed to regard him as an exemplary and
harmless young man, invited the Doctor to
take that trip to Liverpool on board the
Agamenticus, and to spend a week in London or Paris, if he were so inclined, while
the ship was getting ready for the return
voyage.

The proposition nearly blinded Dr. Downs
with its brilliancy. The cabin had been
engaged by Mr. Tredick, and there were
to be no other passengers. There were four
staterooms opening upon the saloon — the
one occupied by the captain was to be given
up to Dr. Downs. The tenor of Mr. Tredick's invitation left the young man no
scruples about accepting it. Mr. Tredick
had said: "On account of my wife and
daughter, I should n't think of crossing

without a medical man on board. I know how valuable a professional man's time is. The favor will be wholly on your side if I can persuade you to go with us." So Dr. Downs agreed to go. To have Miss Tredick all to himself, as it were, for eighteen or twenty days — perhaps twenty-five — was an incredible stroke of fortune. How it would grieve Mr. Cornelius Van Coot, the opulent stockbroker, and that young Delancy Duane, who had caused Newton Downs many an uneasy moment!

"If I am not to have earthly happiness with her," mused Dr. Downs, on his walk home that night from Madison Avenue, "I am to have at least some watery happiness! The dull season is coming on " — he smiled sarcastically as he thought of that — "and all my patients will have retired to their country-seats. Business will not suffer, and I shall escape July and August in town." Then he began making mental vignettes of Miss Tredick in a blue flannel yachting suit, and gave her two small anchors, worked in gold braid, for the standing

collar, and chevrons of the same for the
left coat-sleeve. "How glorious it will be
to promenade the deck in the moonlight
after the old folks have turned in ! I hope
that they will be dreadfully ill, and that we
shall keep dreadfully well. The moment
we pass Sandy Hook Light, overboard goes
Miss Tredick's maid ! . . . What pleasure
it will be to fetch her wraps, and black
Hamburg grapes, and footstools, and iced
lemonades — to sit with her under an awn-
ing, clear aft, with magazines and illustrated
papers " — he instantly resolved to buy out
Brentano — "to lean against the taffrail,
and watch the long emerald sweep of the
waves, and the sweep of Miss Tredick's
eyelashes ! "

It is to be remarked of Miss Tredick's
eyelashes, that they were very long and
very dark, and drooped upon a most health-
ful tint of cheek — neither too rosy nor too
pallid — for she belonged to that later type
of American girl who rides horseback and
is not afraid of a five-mile walk through the
woods and fields. There were great dig-

nity, and delicacy, and strength in her tall
figure; an innocent fearlessness in her
clear, hazel eyes, and, close to, Miss Tredick's eyelashes were worth looking at. It
was young Delancy Duane who said that it
took her half an hour every morning to
disentangle them.

Dr. Downs sat up late that night at the
open window of his office — it was in the
middle of June — reflecting on the endless
pleasant possibilities of the sea voyage.
Would he go no further than Liverpool?
or would he run up to London, and then
over to Paris? In other days he had been
very happy in Paris, in the old Latin
Quarter! He sat there in the silent room,
with no other light than his dreams.

They were not destined to be realized.
That first day at sea promised everything;
then came the rough weather, and then the
terrible storm, which lasted thirty-six hours
or more, and all but wrenched the Agamenticus asunder, leaving her on the fifth
morning, as has been described, a helpless
wreck in the middle of the Atlantic.

During the height of the tempest the
passengers were imprisoned in the cabin,
for it had been necessary to batten down
the hatches. It was so dark below that the
lamp suspended over the cabin table was
kept constantly burning. The heavy seas
on Thursday had put out the fire in the
galley, which was afterward demolished,
and the cook had retreated to some spot
between decks, whence he managed to serve
hot coffee and sandwiches to the saloon at
meal-times. Even this became nearly impracticable after Friday noon.

Mr. and Mrs. Tredick were permanently
confined to their stateroom, and so desper-
ately ill as to be for the most part uncon-
scious of what was taking place. Miss
Tredick's maid, who had been brought
along chiefly to look after Mrs. Tredick,
was in a like condition. Dr. Downs and
Miss Tredick were fair sailors in ordinary
weather; it was the strain on their nerves
that now kept them " dreadfully well."

Neither thought of closing an eye that
fearful Friday night. They passed the

whole night in the saloon, seated opposite each other, with the narrow stationary table, which served as a support, between them. They exchanged scarcely a word as they sat listening to the thud of the tremendous waves that broke over the vessel. Indeed, most of the time speech would have been inaudible amid the roar of the wind, the shuffling tramp of the sailors on the deck, the creak of the strained timbers, and the hundred mysterious, half articulate cries that are wrung from the agony of a ship in a storm at sea.

Miss Tredick was very quiet and serious, but apparently not terrified. If an expression of anxiety now and then came into her face, it was when she glanced toward the stateroom where her mother and father were. The door stood open, and Miss Tredick, by turning slightly in the chair, could see them in their berths. They were lying in a kind of lethargic sleep. Save for a touch of unwonted paleness, and certain traces of weariness about the eyes, Miss Tredick looked as she might have looked sitting, in some very serious mood, in her own room at home. This was courage pure and simple; for the girl was imaginative in a high degree, and it is the imagination that conspires to undermine one's firmness in critical moments. An unimaginative person's indifference to danger is not courage, it is obtuseness. Miss Tredick had the fullest realization of the peril they were in.

There was in her countenance this night a kind of spiritual beauty that seemed new to the young man. "I don't think she ever looked so much like herself before!" was Newton Downs's inward comment once, as he met her gaze across the narrow table. He could hardly keep his eyes away from her.

Dr. Downs's self-possession was not so absolute as Miss Tredick's. He was a brave man, as she was a brave girl, and the fears which unnerved him at intervals were not on his own account. To him his life weighed light in the balance against hers. That all this buoyant womanhood and rare

loveliness should be even remotely menaced
with a cruel death was an intolerable
thought. And the menace was not remote.
There were moments when he wavered in
his faith in the divine goodness. There
were moments, too, when he had it on his
lips to tell Miss Tredick everything that
had been in his mind those last two years.
But here the old pride whispered to him.
Later on, would it not seem as if he had
taken advantage of a fortuitous situation to
make avowals to which she could not well
avoid listening?

It was some time near midnight that the
foremast fell with a great crash. Miss
Tredick involuntarily stretched out one of
her hands to Downs.

" What was that ? "

" A heavy spar, or a topmast, must have
fallen," suggested Downs.

In the lull that followed they could hear
what sounded like axe-strokes dealt in quick
succession. The ship had heeled over
frightfully to port. She held that position
for perhaps twenty minutes, then slowly
righted.

"It was one of the masts," Downs observed; "they have cut it adrift." And Miss Tredick softly withdrew her hand.

After this the lulls grew more frequent and prolonged, and toward daybreak the storm began rapidly to abate. There was very much less motion, and the noises overhead had subsided. The ship's bell, which had made a muffled, intermittent clamor throughout the night, had now given over its tolling. This comparative stillness, succeeding the tumult, seemed to have a poignant quality in it. It was as if the whole world had suddenly stopped, like a clock. The vessel appeared to be making but slight headway. Presently the dawn whitened the stern ports and the little disks of opaque glass let into the deck, and Dr. Downs heard the men at work on the hatches. The long vigil was ended.

"Now go and lie down for an hour or so," he said, rising from the chair with his limbs cramped. "I 'll take a glance at the state of things above. I shall never forget this night, Miss Tredick."

"Nor I," she answered; and she looked so lovely sitting there in the twilight of the cabin, with an illuminated oval port behind her head forming a halo, that the young doctor faltered a second or two on the threshold.

At the top of the companion-way he met Captain Saltus on the point of descending. He was still in his oilskin reefer and overalls, and presented the appearance of a diver who had just been brought exhausted to the surface.

"Good-morning, Captain!" cried Dr. Downs, gayly, exhilarated by a full breath of the fresh sea air and a glimpse of the half-risen sun ploughing up opals and rubies in a low bank of fog stretching to the eastward. "We have weathered it, after all, but by Jove"— Something in the firm-set lines of the Captain's mouth caused the Doctor to leave his sentence unfinished. At the same instant a curious wailing sound reached his ear from the forward part of the ship. "What has happened?" he asked, in a lower voice; for they were close to the companion-way, and the door at the foot of the stair stood open.

" I was just coming to tell you," replied the Captain, gravely, " you and Mr. Tredick."

" Is it anything serious ? "

" Very serious, as serious as can be."

" They must n't hear us below. Come over by the rail. ·What is the matter — has anybody been hurt ? "

" We 've all been hurt, Dr. Downs," returned the Captain, drawing the back of one hand across his wet brows, " every soul of us ! There 's an ugly leak somewhere below the water-line, we don't know where, and ain't likely to know, though the men are tearing up the cargo trying to find out. Perhaps half a dozen seams have started, perhaps a plank. The thing widens. The ship is filling hand over hand, *and the pumps don't work.*"

" But surely the leak will be found ! "

" Dr. Downs," said the Captain, " the old Agamenticus has made her last cruise."

He said this very simply. He had faced

death on almost every known sea, and from his boyhood had looked upon the ocean as his burial place. There he was to lie at last, with his ship, or in a shotted hammock, as the case might be. Such end had been his father's and his grandfather's before him, for he had come of a breed of sea-kings.

" Then we shall have to take to the life-boats ! " cried Downs, breaking from the stupor into which the Captain's announcement had plunged him.

" Two of them were blown out of the lashings last night ; the other two are over yonder."

Dr. Downs's glance followed the pointing of the Captain's finger. Then the young man's chin sank on his breast. " At least we shall die together ! " he said softly to himself.

" I don't know where we are," remarked the Captain, casting his eyes over the lonely expanse of sea. " I 've not been able to take an observation since Wednesday noon. It 's pretty certain that we 've been driven

out of our course, but how far is guess-
work. We're not in the track of vessels,
anyhow. I counted on sighting a sail at
daybreak. It was our only hope, but it
was n't to be. That 's a nasty bit of breeze
off there to the east'ard," he added, irrel-
evantly, following his habit of noting such
detail. Then he recollected the business
that had brought him to the cabin. " Some
of the men for'ard are rigging up a raft ; I
don't myself set any great value on rafts,
as a general thing, but I wish you 'd break
the matter, kind of incidentally, to Mr.
Tredick and the ladies, and tell them to
get ready. There is n't too much time to
lose, Dr. Downs ! "

A figure glided from the companion-
hatch, and passing swiftly by Dr. Downs
halted at the Captain's side.

" I have heard what you said, Captain
Saltus " — Miss Tredick spoke slowly, but
without any tremor in her voice — " and I
am not frightened, you see. I want you to
answer me one question."

" If I can, Miss Tredick."

" How long will it be before — before the end comes ? "

" Well, miss, the wind has died away, and the sea is getting smoother every second. Mr. Bowlsby thinks he will be able to launch the raft within three quarters of an hour. Then there's the ship-stores " —

" Yes ! yes ! — but how long ? "

" Before we leave the ship, miss ? "

" No, before the ship sinks ! "

" That I can't say. She may keep afloat two or three hours, if the wind does n't freshen."

" And if the wind freshens ? "

" It would be lively work, miss."

" You are convinced, then, that we are irrevocably lost ? "

" Well," returned the Captain, embarrassed by the unexpected composure of the girl, " I would never say that. There's the raft. There is generally a chance of being picked up. Besides, we are always in God's world ! "

Miss Tredick bowed her head, and let her hand rest gently for an instant on the

Captain's coat-sleeve. In that touch was a furtive and pathetic farewell.

" Miss Tredick," cried the Captain, as he lifted his cap respectfully, " damn me if I 'm not proud to sink with so brave a lady, and any man might well be ! You 're a lesson to those Portuguese, with their leaden images, caterwauling up there in the bows ! "

" Now I would like to speak a moment with Dr. Downs," said Miss Tredick, half hesitatingly.

As the Captain slowly walked forward among the crew, there was a dash of salt spray on his cheek. The girl paused, and looked after him with a quick, indescribable expression of tenderness in her eyes. Two intrepid souls, moving on diverse planes in this lower sphere, had met in one swift instant of recognition !

During the short dialogue between Captain Saltus and Miss Tredick, Newton Downs had stood leaning against the rail, a few feet distant. As he stood there he noticed that the ship was gradually settling.

Until the night before, the idea of death — of death close to, immediate — had never come to him; it had been always something vague, a thing possible, perhaps certain, after years and years. It had been a very real thing to him that night in the storm, yet still indistinct so far as touched him personally; for his thoughts had been less of himself than of Miss Tredick. His thought now was wholly of her. What should be done? Would it not be better to go down in the vessel than to drift about the Atlantic for days and days on a fragile raft, and endure a thousand deaths? When he contemplated the possible horror of such brief reprieve, his heart turned cold. If it was decided to take to the raft, he would pray that another blow, such as the Captain seemed to predict, might speedily come to end their suffering. The Captain himself had plainly resolved to sink with the ship. Would not that be the more merciful fate for all of them? Had not the thought occurred to Miss Tredick, too?

" Dr. Downs."

The young man raised his head, and saw Miss Tredick standing in front of him. There was a noticeable alteration in her manner; it lacked something of the self-possession it had had while she was address-ing the Captain, and her lips were nearly colorless. "Is she losing her splendid courage?" Downs asked himself, with a pang.

"There may not be another opportunity for me to speak with you alone," she said hurriedly, "here or on the raft. How cruel it all seems! The world we knew has sud-denly and strangely come to an end for us. I could not say to you in that world what I wish to say to you now. You, too, did not speak your thoughts to me there, and the reason of your silence was unworthy of us both" — Dr. Downs gave a little start, and made a motion to interrupt her, but she stopped him with an imploring gesture. "No, you must listen, for these are my dy-ing words. You were blind — oh, so blind! You did not see me as I was, you did not understand, for I think I loved you from that first day " — then, with a piteous quiver of the lip, she added — " and I shall love you all the rest of my life ! "

The young man's first impulse was to kneel at her feet, but the tall, slight figure was now drooping before him. He leaned forward, and took the girl in his arms. She rested her cheek on his shoulder, with her eyes closed. So they stood there, silently, in the red sunrise. Whether life lasted a minute or a century was all one to those two lovers on the sinking ship.

The hammering of the men at work on the raft had ceased, and the strange silence that fell upon the vessel was emphasized rather than broken by the intermittent lamentations of the Portuguese sailors crowded into the bow of the ship. Captain Saltus, with a curious expression in his face, leaned against the capstan, watching them.

Suddenly there was a rush of feet, followed by confused cries on the forecastle-deck; a man had shouted something, the import of which did not instantly reach the little group aft.

"Where away?" cried the second officer, leaping into the lower shrouds.

"On the starboard bow, sir! The fog's been hiding her."

"Where's the glass? — can you make her out?"

"I think it's an Inman liner, sir — she is signaling to us!"

"Thank God!"